AN
EVERGREEN
CHRISTMAS

AN EVERGREEN CHRISTMAS

TREASURED CLASSICS
FOR THE YULETIDE SEASON

DEXTERITY
NASHVILLE

604 Magnolia Lane
Nashville, TN 37211

Printed in the United States of America.

First edition: 2022
10 9 8 7 6 5 4 3 2 1

ISBN: 978-1-947297-51-7 (Hardcover)
ISBN: 978-1-947297-52-4 (E-book)

Publisher's Cataloging-in-Publication Data

Title: An evergreen Christmas : treasured classics for the Yuletide season.
Description: Nashville, TN: Dexterity, 2022.
Identifiers: ISBN: 978-1-947297-51-7 (hardcover) | 978-1-947297-52-4 (ebook)
Subjects: LCSH Christmas--Literary collections. | Christmas stories. | Christmas poetry. | Christmas music. | BISAC RELIGION / Holidays / Christmas & Advent | FICTION / Holidays | FICTION / Christian / Classic & Allegory | FICTION / Anthologies (multiple authors) | FICTION / Classics
Classification: LCC PZ5 .E84 2022 | DDC 808.8/033--dc23

Cover and interior design by Sarah Siegand

To all those dreaming of an evergreen Christmas

Contents

CONTENTS

TREASURED CLASSICS
FOR THE YULETIDE SEASON

It Came Upon the Midnight Clear

Edmund H. Sears

It came upon the midnight clear,

that glorious song of old,

from angels bending near the earth

to touch their harps of gold:

"Peace on the earth, good will to men,

from heaven's all-gracious King."

The world in solemn stillness lay,

to hear the angels sing.

Still through the cloven skies they come

with peaceful wings unfurled,

and still their heavenly music floats
o'er all the weary world;
above its sad and lowly plains,
they bend on hovering wing,
and ever o'er its Babel sounds
the blessed angels sing.

Yet with the woes of sin and strife
the world has suffered long;
beneath the angel strain have rolled
two thousand years of wrong;
and man, at war with man, hears not
the love-song which they bring;
oh, hush the noise, ye men of strife
and hear the angels sing.

And ye, beneath life's crushing load,
whose forms are bending low,
who toil along the climbing way
with painful steps and slow,
look now! for glad and golden hours
come swiftly on the wing.
O rest beside the weary road,
and hear the angels sing!

For lo! the days are hastening on,
by prophet seen of old,
when with the ever-circling years
shall come the time foretold
when peace shall over all the earth
its ancient splendors fling,
and the whole world send back the song
which now the angels sing.

Tilly's Christmas

Louisa May Alcott

"I'm so glad to-morrow is Christmas, because I'm going to have lots of presents."

"So am I glad, though I don't expect any presents but a pair of mittens."

"And so am I; but I shan't have any presents at all."

As the three little girls trudged home from school they said these things, and as Tilly spoke, both the others looked at her with pity and some surprise, for she spoke cheerfully, and they wondered how she could be happy when she was so poor she could have no presents on Christmas.

"Don't you wish you could find a purse full of money

right here in the path?" said Kate, the child who was going to have "lots of presents."

"Oh, don't I, if I could keep it honestly!" and Tilly's eyes shone at the very thought.

"What would you buy?" asked Bessy, rubbing her cold hands, and longing for her mittens.

"I'd buy a pair of large, warm blankets, a load of wood, a shawl for mother, and a pair of shoes for me; and if there was enough left, I'd give Bessy a new hat, and then she needn't wear Ben's old felt one," answered Tilly.

The girls laughed at that; but Bessy pulled the funny hat over her ears, and said she was much obliged but she'd rather have candy.

"Let's look, and maybe we *can* find a purse. People are always going about with money at Christmas time, and some one may lose it here," said Kate.

So, as they went along the snowy road, they looked about them, half in earnest, half in fun. Suddenly Tilly sprang forward, exclaiming—

"I see it! I've found it!"

The others followed, but all stopped disappointed; for it wasn't a purse, it was only a little bird. It lay upon the snow with its wings spread and feebly fluttering, as if too weak to fly. Its little feet were benumbed with cold; its once

6

bright eyes were dull with pain, and instead of a blithe song, it could only utter a faint chirp, now and then, as if crying for help.

"Nothing but a stupid old robin; how provoking!" cried Kate, sitting down to rest.

"I shan't touch it. I found one once, and took care of it, and the ungrateful thing flew away the minute it was well," said Bessy, creeping under Kate's shawl, and putting her hands under her chin to warm them.

"Poor little birdie! How pitiful he looks, and how glad he must be to see some one coming to help him! I'll take him up gently, and carry him home to mother. Don't be frightened, dear, I'm your friend"; and Tilly knelt down in the snow, stretching her hand to the bird, with the tenderest pity in her face.

Kate and Bessy laughed.

"Don't stop for that thing; it's getting late and cold: let's go on and look for the purse," they said moving away.

"You wouldn't leave it to die!" cried Tilly. "I'd rather have the bird than the money, so I shan't look any more. The purse wouldn't be mine, and I should only be tempted to keep it; but this poor thing will thank and love me, and I'm *so* glad I came in time."

Gently lifting the bird, Tilly felt its tiny cold claws cling to her hand, and saw its dim eyes brighten as it nestled down with a grateful chirp.

"Now I've got a Christmas present after all," she said, smiling, as they walked on. "I always wanted a bird, and this one will be such a pretty pet for me."

"He'll fly away the first chance he gets, and die anyhow; so you'd better not waste your time over him," said Bessy.

"He can't pay you for taking care of him, and my mother says it isn't worth while to help folks that can't help us," added Kate.

"My mother says, 'Do as you'd be done by'; and I'm sure I'd like any one to help me if I was dying of cold and hunger. 'Love your neighbour as yourself,' is another of her sayings. This bird is my little neighbour, and I'll love him and care for him, as I often wish our rich neighbour would love and care for us," answered Tilly, breathing her warm breath over the benumbed bird, who looked up at her with confiding eyes, quick to feel and know a friend.

"What a funny girl you are," said Kate; "caring for that silly bird, and talking about loving your neighbour in that sober way. Mr. King don't care a bit for you, and never will, though he knows how poor you are; so I don't think your plan amounts to much."

"I believe it, though; and shall do my part, any way.

Good-night. I hope you'll have a merry Christmas, and lots of pretty things," answered Tilly, as they parted.

Her eyes were full, and she felt so poor as she went on alone toward the little old house where she lived. It would have been so pleasant to know that she was going to have some of the pretty things all children love to find in their full stockings on Christmas morning. And pleasanter still to have been able to give her mother something nice. So many comforts were needed, and there was no hope of getting them; for they could barely get food and fire.

"Never mind, birdie, we'll make the best of what we have, and be merry in spite of every thing. *You* shall have a happy Christmas, any way; and I know God won't forget us if every one else does."

She stopped a minute to wipe her eyes, and lean her cheek against the bird's soft breast, finding great comfort in the little creature, though it could only love her, nothing more.

"See, mother, what a nice present I've found," she cried, going in with a cheery face that was like sunshine in the dark room.

"I'm glad of that, dearie; for I haven't been able to get my little girl anything but a rosy apple. Poor bird! Give it some of your warm bread and milk."

"Why, mother, what a big bowlful! I'm afraid you gave me all the milk," said Tilly, smiling over the nice, steaming supper that stood ready for her.

"I've had plenty, dear. Sit down and dry your wet feet, and put the bird in my basket on this warm flannel."

Tilly peeped into the closet and saw nothing there but dry bread.

"Mother's given me all the milk, and is going without her tea, 'cause she knows I'm hungry. Now I'll surprise her, and she shall have a good supper too. She is going to split wood, and I'll fix it while she's gone."

So Tilly put down the old tea-pot, carefully poured out a part of the milk, and from her pocket produced a great, plummy bun, that one of the school-children had given her, and she had saved for her mother. A slice of the dry bread was nicely toasted, and the bit of butter set by for her put on it. When her mother came in there was the table drawn up in a warm place, a hot cup of tea ready, and Tilly and birdie waiting for her.

Such a poor little supper, and yet such a happy one; for love, charity, and contentment were guests there, and that Christmas eve was a blither one than that up at the great house, where lights shone, fires blazed, a great tree glittered, and music sounded, as the children danced and played.

"We must go to bed early, for we've only wood enough to last over to-morrow. I shall be paid for my work the day after, and then we can get some," said Tilly's mother, as they sat by the fire.

"If my bird was only a fairy bird, and would give us three wishes, how nice it would be! Poor dear, he can't give me any thing; but it's no matter," answered Tilly, looking at the robin, who lay in the basket with his head under his wing, a mere little feathery bunch.

'He can give you one thing, Tilly—the pleasure of doing good. That is one of the sweetest things in life; and the poor can enjoy it as well as the rich.'

As her mother spoke, with her tired hand softly stroking her little daughter's hair, Tilly suddenly started and pointed to the window, saying, in a frightened whisper—

"I saw a face—a man's face, looking in! It's gone now; but I truly saw it."

"Some traveller attracted by the light perhaps. I'll go and see." And Tilly's mother went to the door.

No one was there. The wind blew cold, the stars shone, the snow lay white on field and wood, and the Christmas moon was glittering in the sky.

"What sort of a face was it?" asked Tilly's mother, coming back.

"A pleasant sort of face, I think; but I was so startled I don't quite know what it was like. I wish we had a curtain there,' said Tilly.

"I like to have our light shine out in the evening, for the road is dark and lonely just here, and the twinkle of our lamp is pleasant to people's eyes as they go by. We can do so little for our neighbours, I am glad to cheer the way for them. Now put these poor old shoes to dry, and go to bed, dearie; I'll come soon."

Tilly went, taking her bird with her to sleep in his basket near by, lest he should be lonely in the night.

Soon the little house was dark and still, and no one saw the Christmas spirits at their work that night.

When Tilly opened the door next morning, she gave a loud cry, clapped her hands, and then stood still; quite speechless with wonder and delight. There, before the door, lay a great pile of wood, all ready to burn, a big bundle and a basket, with a lovely nosegay of winter roses, holly, and evergreen tied to the handle.

"Oh, mother! did the fairies do it?" cried Tilly, pale with her happiness, as she seized the basket, while her mother took in the bundle.

"Yes, dear, the best and dearest fairy in the world, called 'Charity.' She walks abroad at Christmas time, does beautiful deeds like this, and does not stay to be thanked," answered her mother with full eyes, as she undid the parcel.

There they were—the warm, thick blankets, the comfortable shawls, the new shoes, and, best of all, a pretty winter hat for Bessy. The basket was full of good things to eat, and on the flowers lay a paper, saying—

"For the little girl who loves her neighbour as herself."

"Mother, I really think my bird is a fairy bird, and all these splendid things come from him," said Tilly, laughing and crying with joy.

It really did seem so, for as she spoke, the robin flew to the table, hopped to the nosegay, and perching among the roses, began to chirp with all his little might. The sun streamed in on flowers, bird, and happy child, and no one saw a shadow glide away from the window; no one ever knew that Mr. King had seen and heard the little girls the night before, or dreamed that the rich neighbour had learned a lesson from the poor neighbour.

And Tilly's bird *was* a fairy bird; for by her love and tenderness to the helpless thing, she brought good gifts to herself, happiness to the unknown giver of them, and a faithful little friend who did not fly away, but stayed with her till the snow was gone, making summer for her in the winter-time.

Johnnie's Christmas

Libbie C. Baer

Papa and mama, and baby and Dot,
Willie and me—the whole of the lot
Of us all went over in Bimberlie's sleigh,
To grandmama's house on Christmas day.

Covered with robes on the soft cushioned seat,
With heads well wrapped up and hot bricks to
   our feet,
And two prancing horses, tho' ten miles away,
The ride was quite short, on that bright
   Christmas day.

When all were tucked in and the driver said
    "Go!"
The horses just flew o'er the white, shining snow;
The town it slipped by us and meadow and tree,
And farm house till grandmama's house we did see.

Grandmama was watching for us, there's no
    doubt;
She soon come to meet us, and helped us all out;
And kissin' and huggin' said how we boys
    growed,
And big as our papa we'd soon be, she knowed.
And Dot she called handsome and said: "Ah! I
    guess
Grandmama's woman has got a new dress."
And said that the baby was pretty and smart;
"Dod b'ess it and love its own sweet 'ittle heart."

And O, the red apples, and pop-corn on strings;
And balls of it, too, and nuts, candy and things;
And O, such a dinner and such pumpkin pie;
I eat and I eat till I thought I would die.

And grandmama urgin', "Now, Johnnie, my man,

I wants you to eat; just eat all you can."
When I eat all I could then I eat a lots more,
And I didn't feel good as I had felt before.

At last it came time for us all to go back,
And into the sleigh again, all of us pack;
With grandmama kissin' and sayin' good byes,
With smiles on her lips, but the tears in her eyes.

We seemed much more crowded, and Bimberlie's
    sleigh
Kept jerkin' and hurtin' me most all the way;
The robes were so stuffy I couldn't get breath,
And Dot and the baby most squeezed me to
    death.
All night I kept tumblin' and tossin', ma said,
And frowed all the cover half off of the bed;
I dreamed of roast turkey and pop-corn and pie,
And fruit cake and candy, *piled up to the sky!*

And I dreamed I was sick and just lookin' at it,
A wantin' and yet I could not eat a bit;
And grandmama urgin', "Now, Johnnie, my man,
I want you to eat, just eat *all you can.*"

A Christmas Dinner

Charles Dickens

Christmas time! That man must be a misanthrope indeed, in whose breast something like a jovial feeling is not roused—in whose mind some pleasant associations are not awakened—by the recurrence of Christmas. There are people who will tell you that Christmas is not to them what it used to be; that each succeeding Christmas has found some cherished hope, or happy prospect, of the year before, dimmed or passed away; that the present only serves to remind them of reduced circumstances and straitened incomes—of the feasts they once bestowed on hollow friends, and of the cold looks that meet them now, in adversity and misfortune. Never heed such dismal reminiscences. There are few men who have lived long enough in the world, who cannot call up such thoughts any day in the year. Then do not select the merriest of the three hundred and sixty-five for your doleful recollections, but draw your chair nearer the blazing fire—fill the glass and send round the song—and if your room be smaller than it was a dozen years ago, or if your glass be filled with reeking punch, instead of sparkling wine, put a good face on the matter, and empty it off-hand, and fill another, and troll off the old ditty you used to sing, and thank God it's no worse. Look on the merry faces of your children (if you have any) as they sit round the fire. One little seat may be empty; one slight form that gladdened the father's heart, and roused the mother's pride to look upon, may not be there. Dwell not upon the past; think not that one short year ago, the fair child now resolving into dust, sat before you, with the bloom of health upon its cheek, and the gaiety of infancy in its joyous eye. Reflect upon your present blessings—of which every man has many—not on your past misfortunes, of which all men have some. Fill your glass again, with a merry face and contented heart. Our life on it, but your Christmas shall be merry, and your new year a happy one!

Who can be insensible to the outpourings of good feeling, and the honest interchange of affectionate attachment, which abound at this season of the year? A Christmas family-party! We know nothing in nature more delightful! There seems a magic in the very name of Christmas. Petty jealousies and discords are forgotten; social feelings are awakened, in bosoms to which they have long been strangers; father and son, or brother and sister, who have met and passed with averted gaze, or a look of cold recognition, for months before, proffer and return the cordial embrace, and bury their past animosities in their present happiness. Kindly hearts that have yearned towards each other, but have been withheld by false notions of pride and self-dignity, are again reunited, and all is kindness and benevolence! Would that Christmas lasted the whole year through (as it ought), and that the prejudices and passions which deform our better nature, were never called into action among those to whom they should ever be strangers!

The Christmas family-party that we mean, is not a mere assemblage of relations, got up at a week or two's notice, originating this year, having no family precedent in the last, and not likely to be repeated in the next. No. It is an annual gathering of all the accessible members of the family, young or old, rich or poor; and all the children look forward to it, for two months beforehand, in a fever of anticipation. Formerly, it was held at grandpapa's; but grandpapa getting old, and grandmamma getting old too, and rather infirm, they have given up house-keeping, and domesticated themselves with uncle George; so, the party always takes place at uncle George's house, but grandmamma sends in most of the good things, and grandpapa always WILL toddle down, all the way to Newgate-market, to buy the turkey, which he engages a porter to bring home behind him in triumph, always insisting on the man's being rewarded with a glass of spirits, over and above his hire, to drink "a merry Christmas and a happy new year" to aunt George. As to grandmamma, she is very secret and mysterious for two or three days beforehand, but not sufficiently so, to prevent rumours getting afloat that she has purchased a beautiful new cap with pink ribbons for each of the servants, together with sundry books, and pen-knives, and pencil-cases, for the younger branches; to say nothing of divers secret additions to the order originally given by aunt George at the pastry-cook's, such as another dozen of mince-pies for the dinner, and a large plum-cake for the children.

On Christmas-eve, grandmamma is always in excellent spirits, and after employing all the children, during the day, in stoning the plums, and all that, insists, regularly every year, on uncle George coming down into the kitchen, taking off his coat, and stirring the pudding for half an hour or so, which uncle George good-humouredly does, to the vociferous delight of the children and servants. The evening concludes with a glorious game of blind-man's-buff, in an early stage of which grandpapa takes great care to be caught, in order that he may have an opportunity of displaying his dexterity.

On the following morning, the old couple, with as many of the children as the pew will hold, go to church in great state: leaving aunt George at home dusting decanters and filling casters, and uncle George carrying bottles into the dining-parlour, and calling for corkscrews, and getting into everybody's way.

When the church-party return to lunch, grandpapa produces a small sprig of mistletoe from his pocket, and tempts the boys to kiss their little cousins under it—a proceeding which affords both the boys and the old gentleman unlimited satisfaction, but which rather outrages grandmamma's ideas of decorum, until grandpapa says, that when he was just thirteen years and three months old, HE kissed grandmamma under a mistletoe too, on which the children clap their hands, and laugh very heartily, as do aunt George and uncle George; and grandmamma looks pleased, and says, with a benevolent smile, that grandpapa was an impudent young dog, on which the children laugh very heartily again, and grandpapa more heartily than any of them.

But all these diversions are nothing to the subsequent excitement when grandmamma in a high cap, and slate-coloured silk gown; and grandpapa with a beautifully plaited shirt-frill, and white neckerchief; seat themselves on one side of the drawing-room fire, with uncle George's children and little cousins innumerable, seated in the front, waiting the arrival of the expected visitors. Suddenly a hackney-coach is heard to stop, and uncle George, who has been looking out of the window, exclaims "Here's Jane!" on which the children rush to the door, and helter-skelter down stairs; and uncle Robert and aunt Jane, and the dear little baby, and the nurse, and the whole party, are ushered up stairs amidst tumultuous shouts of "Oh, my!" from the children, and frequently repeated warnings not to hurt baby from the nurse. And grandpapa takes the child, and grandmamma kisses her daughter, and the confusion of this first entry has scarcely subsided, when some other aunts and uncles with more cousins arrive, and the grown-up cousins flirt with each other, and so do the little cousins too, for that matter, and nothing is to be heard but a confused din of talking, laughing, and merriment.

A hesitating double knock at the street-door, heard during a momentary pause in the conversation, excites a general inquiry of "Who's that?" and two or three children, who have been standing at the window, announce in a low voice, that it's "poor aunt Margaret." Upon which, aunt George leaves the room to welcome the new-comer; and grandmamma draws herself up, rather stiff and stately; for Margaret married a poor man without her consent, and poverty not being a sufficiently weighty punishment for her offence, has been discarded by her friends, and debarred the society of her dearest relatives. But Christmas has come round, and the unkind feelings that have struggled against better dispositions during the year, have melted away before its genial influence, like half-formed ice beneath the morning sun. It is not difficult in a moment of angry feeling for a parent to denounce a disobedient child; but, to banish her at a period of general good-will and hilarity, from the hearth, round which she has sat on so many anniversaries of the same day, expanding by slow degrees from infancy to girlhood, and then bursting, almost imperceptibly, into a woman, is widely different. The air of conscious rectitude, and cold forgiveness, which the old lady has assumed, sits ill upon her; and when the poor girl is led in by her sister, pale in looks and broken in hope—not from poverty, for that

25

she could bear, but from the consciousness of undeserved neglect, and unmerited unkindness—it is easy to see how much of it is assumed. A momentary pause succeeds; the girl breaks suddenly from her sister and throws herself, sobbing, on her mother's neck. The father steps hastily forward, and takes her husband's hand. Friends crowd round to offer their hearty congratulations, and happiness and harmony again prevail.

As to the dinner, it's perfectly delightful—nothing goes wrong, and everybody is in the very best of spirits, and disposed to please and be pleased. Grandpapa relates a circumstantial account of the purchase of the turkey, with a slight digression relative to the purchase of previous turkeys, on former Christmas-days, which grandmamma corroborates in the minutest particular. Uncle George tells stories, and carves poultry, and takes wine, and jokes with the children at the side-table, and winks at the cousins that are making love, or being made love to, and exhilarates everybody with his good humour and hospitality; and when, at last, a stout servant staggers in with a gigantic pudding, with a sprig of holly in the top, there is such a laughing, and shouting, and clapping of little chubby hands, and kicking up of fat dumpy legs, as can only be equalled by the applause with which the astonishing feat of pouring lighted brandy into mince-pies, is received by the younger visitors. Then the dessert!—and the wine!—and the fun! Such beautiful speeches, and SUCH songs, from aunt Margaret's husband, who turns out to be such a nice man, and SO attentive to grandmamma! Even grandpapa not only sings his annual song with unprecedented vigour, but on being honoured with an unanimous ENCORE, according to annual custom, actually comes out with a new one which nobody but grandmamma ever heard before; and a young scapegrace of a cousin, who has been in some disgrace with the old people, for certain heinous sins of omission and commission—neglecting to call, and persisting in drinking Burton Ale—astonishes everybody into convulsions of laughter by volunteering the most extraordinary comic songs that ever were heard. And thus the evening passes, in a strain of rational good-will and cheerfulness, doing more to awaken the sympathies of every member of the party in behalf of his neighbour, and to perpetuate their good feeling during the ensuing year, than half the homilies that have ever been written, by half the Divines that have ever lived.

A Visit from St. Nicholas

('Twas the Night Before Christmas)

Clement Clarke Moore

'Twas the night before Christmas, when all
    through the house
Not a creature was stirring, not even a mouse;
The stockings were hung by the chimney with
    care,
In hopes that St. Nicholas soon would be there;
The children were nestled all snug in their beds,
While visions of sugar-plums danced in their
    heads;
And mamma in her 'kerchief, and I in my cap,
Had just settled our brains for a long winter's nap,

When out on the lawn there arose such a clatter,

I sprang from the bed to see what was the matter.

Away to the window I flew like a flash,

Tore open the shutters and threw up the sash.

The moon on the breast of the new-fallen snow

Gave the lustre of mid-day to objects below,

When, what to my wondering eyes should

    appear,

But a miniature sleigh, and eight tiny reindeer,

With a little old driver, so lively and quick,

I knew in a moment it must be St. Nick.

More rapid than eagles his coursers they came,

And he whistled, and shouted, and called them

    by name;

"Now, *Dasher*! now, *Dancer*! now, *Prancer* and

    Vixen!

On, *Comet*! on, *Cupid*! on, *Donner* and *Blitzen*!

To the top of the porch! to the top of the wall!

Now dash away! dash away! dash away all!"

As dry leaves that before the wild hurricane fly,

When they meet with an obstacle, mount to the sky;

So up to the house-top the coursers they flew,

With the sleigh full of Toys, and St. Nicholas too.

And then, in a twinkling, I heard on the roof

The prancing and pawing of each little hoof.

As I drew in my head, and was turning around,

Down the chimney St. Nicholas came with a
    bound.

He was dressed all in fur, from his head to his
    foot,

And his clothes were all tarnished with ashes and
    soot;

A bundle of Toys he had flung on his back,

And he looked like a pedler just opening his pack.

His eyes—how they twinkled! his dimples how
    merry!

His cheeks were like roses, his nose like a cherry!

His droll little mouth was drawn up like a bow

And the beard of his chin was as white as the
    snow;

The stump of a pipe he held tight in his teeth,

And the smoke it encircled his head like a wreath;

He had a broad face and a little round belly,

That shook when he laughed, like a bowlful of
    jelly.

He was chubby and plump, a right jolly old elf,

And I laughed when I saw him, in spite of myself;

A wink of his eye and a twist of his head,

Soon gave me to know I had nothing to dread;

He spoke not a word, but went straight to his
work,

And filled all the stockings; then turned with a
jerk,

And laying his finger aside of his nose,

And giving a nod, up the chimney he rose;

He sprang to his sleigh, to his team gave a whistle,

And away they all flew like the down of a thistle,

But I heard him exclaim, ere he drove out of
sight,

"Happy Christmas to all, and to all a good-night."

CLORINDA'S GIFTS

L. M. Montgomery

"It is a dreadful thing to be poor a fortnight before Christmas," said Clorinda, with the mournful sigh of seventeen years.

Aunt Emmy smiled. Aunt Emmy was sixty, and spent the hours she didn't spend in a bed, on a sofa or in a wheel chair; but Aunt Emmy was never heard to sigh.

"I suppose it is worse then than at any other time," she admitted.

That was one of the nice things about Aunt Emmy. She always sympathized and understood.

"I'm worse than poor this Christmas . . . I'm stony broke," said Clorinda dolefully. "My spell of fever in the summer and the consequent doctor's bills have cleaned out my coffers completely. Not a single Christmas present can I give. And I did so want to give some little thing to each of my dearest people. But I simply can't afford it . . . that's the hateful, ugly truth."

Clorinda sighed again.

"The gifts which money can purchase are not the only ones we can give," said Aunt Emmy gently, "nor the best, either."

"Oh, I know it's nicer to give something of your own work," agreed Clorinda, "but materials for fancy work cost too. That kind of gift is just as much out of the question for me as any other."

"That was not what I meant," said Aunt Emmy.

"What did you mean, then?" asked Clorinda, looking puzzled.

Aunt Emmy smiled.

"Suppose you think out my meaning for yourself," she said. "That would be better than if I explained it. Besides, I don't think I could explain it. Take the beautiful line of a beautiful poem to help you in your thinking out: 'The gift without the giver is bare.'"

"I'd put it the other way and say, 'The giver without the gift is bare,'" said Clorinda, with a grimace. "That is my predicament exactly. Well, I hope by next Christmas I'll not be quite bankrupt. I'm going into Mr. Callender's store down at Murraybridge in February. He has offered me the place, you know."

"Won't your aunt miss you terribly?" said Aunt Emmy gravely.

Clorinda flushed. There was a note in Aunt Emmy's voice that disturbed her.

"Oh, yes, I suppose she will," she answered hurriedly. "But she'll get used to it very soon. And I will be home every Saturday night, you know. I'm dreadfully tired of being poor, Aunt Emmy, and now that I have a chance to earn something for myself I mean to take it. I can help Aunt Mary, too. I'm to get four dollars a week."

"I think she would rather have your companionship than a part of your salary, Clorinda," said Aunt Emmy. "But of course you must decide for yourself, dear. It is hard to be poor. I know it. I am poor."

"You poor!" said Clorinda, kissing her. "Why, you are the richest woman I know, Aunt Emmy—rich in love and goodness and contentment."

"And so are you, dearie . . . rich in youth and health and happiness and ambition. Aren't they all worth while?"

"Of course they are," laughed Clorinda. "Only, unfortunately, Christmas gifts can't be coined out of them."

"Did you ever try?" asked Aunt Emmy. "Think out that question, too, in your thinking out, Clorinda."

"Well, I must say bye-bye and run home. I feel cheered up—you always cheer people up, Aunt Emmy. How grey it is outdoors. I do hope we'll have snow soon. Wouldn't it be jolly to have a white Christmas? We always have such faded brown Decembers."

Clorinda lived just across the road from Aunt Emmy in a tiny white house behind some huge willows. But Aunt Mary lived there too—the only relative Clorinda had, for Aunt Emmy wasn't really her aunt at all. Clorinda had always lived with Aunt Mary ever since she could remember.

Clorinda went home and upstairs to her little room under the eaves, where the great bare willow boughs were branching athwart her windows. She was thinking over what Aunt Emmy had said about Christmas gifts and giving.

"I'm sure I don't know what she could have meant," pondered Clorinda. "I do wish I could find out if it would help me any. I'd love to remember a few of my friends at least. There's Miss Mitchell . . . she's been so good to me all this year and helped me so much with my studies. And there's Mrs. Martin out in Manitoba. If I could only send her something! She must be so lonely out there. And Aunt Emmy herself, of course; and poor old Aunt Kitty down the lane; and Aunt Mary and, yes—Florence too, although she did treat me so meanly. I shall never feel the same to her again. But she gave me a present last Christmas, and so out of mere politeness I ought to give her something."

Clorinda stopped short suddenly. She had just remembered that she would not have liked to say that last sentence to Aunt Emmy. Therefore, there was something wrong about it. Clorinda had long ago learned that there was sure to be something wrong in anything that could not be said to Aunt Emmy. So she stopped to think it over.

Clorinda puzzled over Aunt Emmy's meaning for four days and part of three nights. Then all at once it came to her. Or if it wasn't Aunt Emmy's meaning it was a very good meaning in itself, and it grew clearer and expanded in meaning during the days that followed, although at first Clorinda shrank a little from some of the conclusions to which it led her.

"I've solved the problem of my Christmas giving for this year," she told Aunt Emmy. "I have some things to give after all. Some of them quite costly, too; that is, they will cost me something, but I know I'll be better off and richer after I've paid the price. That is what Mr. Grierson would call a paradox, isn't it? I'll explain all about it to you on Christmas Day."

On Christmas Day, Clorinda went over to Aunt Emmy's. It was a faded brown Christmas after all, for the snow had not come. But Clorinda did not mind; there was such joy in her heart that she thought it the most delightful Christmas Day that ever dawned.

She put the queer cornery armful she carried down on the kitchen floor before she went into the sitting room. Aunt Emmy was lying on the sofa before the fire, and Clorinda sat down beside her.

"I've come to tell you all about it," she said.

Aunt Emmy patted the hand that was in her own.

"From your face, dear girl, it will be pleasant hearing and telling," she said.

Clorinda nodded.

"Aunt Emmy, I thought for days over your meaning . . . thought until I was dizzy. And then one evening it just came to me, without any thinking at all, and I knew that I could give some gifts after all. I thought of something new every day for a week. At first I didn't think I could give some of them, and then I thought how selfish I was. I would have been willing to pay any amount of money for gifts if I had had it, but I wasn't willing to pay what I had. I got over that, though, Aunt Emmy. Now I'm going to tell you what I did give.

"First, there was my teacher, Miss Mitchell. I gave her one of father's books. I have so many of his, you know, so that I wouldn't miss one; but still it was one I loved very much, and so I felt that that love made it worth while. That is, I felt that on second thought. At first, Aunt Emmy, I thought I would be ashamed to offer Miss Mitchell a shabby old book, worn with much reading and all marked over with father's notes and pencillings. I was afraid she would think it queer of me to give her such a present. And yet somehow it seemed to me that it was better than something brand new and un-mellowed—that old book which father had loved and which I loved. So I gave it to her, and she understood. I think it pleased her so much, the real meaning in it. She said it was like being given something out of another's heart and life.

"Then you know Mrs. Martin . . . last year she was Miss Hope, my dear Sunday School teacher. She married a home missionary, and they are in a lonely part of the west. Well, I wrote her a letter. Not just an ordinary letter; dear me, no. I took a whole day to write it, and you should have seen the postmistress's eyes stick out when I mailed it. I just told her everything that had happened in Greenvale since she went away. I made it as newsy and cheerful and loving as I possibly could. Everything bright and funny I could think of went into it.

"The next was old Aunt Kitty. You know she was my nurse when I was a baby, and she's very fond of me. But, well, you know, Aunt Emmy, I'm ashamed to confess it, but really I've never found Aunt Kitty very entertaining, to put it mildly. She is always glad when I go to see her, but I've never gone except when I couldn't help it. She is very deaf, and rather dull and stupid, you know. Well, I gave her a whole day. I took my knitting yesterday, and sat with her the whole time and just talked and talked. I told her all the Greenvale news and gossip and everything else I thought she'd like to hear. She was so pleased and proud; she told me when I came away that she hadn't had such a nice time for years.

"Then there was . . . Florence. You know, Aunt Emmy, we were always intimate friends until last year. Then Florence once told Rose Watson something I had told her in confidence. I found it out and I was so hurt. I couldn't forgive Florence, and I told her plainly I could never be a real friend to her again. Florence felt badly, because she really did love me, and she asked me to forgive her, but it seemed as if I couldn't. Well, Aunt Emmy, that was my Christmas gift to her . . . my forgiveness. I went down last night and just put my arms around her and told her that I loved her as much as ever and wanted to be real close friends again.

"I gave Aunt Mary her gift this morning. I told her I wasn't going to Murraybridge, that I just meant to stay home with her. She was so glad—and I'm glad, too, now that I've decided so."

"Your gifts have been real gifts, Clorinda," said Aunt Emmy. "Something of you—the best of you—went into each of them."

Clorinda went out and brought her cornery armful in.

"I didn't forget you, Aunt Emmy," she said, as she unpinned the paper.

There was a rosebush—Clorinda's own pet rosebush—all snowed over with fragrant blossoms.

Aunt Emmy loved flowers. She put her finger under one of the roses and kissed it.

"It's as sweet as yourself, dear child," she said tenderly. "And it will be a joy to me all through the lonely winter days. You've found out the best meaning of Christmas giving, haven't you, dear?"

"Yes, thanks to you, Aunt Emmy," said Clorinda softly.

Music on Christmas Morning

Anne Brontë

Music I love—but never strain
Could kindle raptures so divine,
So grief assuage, so conquer pain,
And rouse this pensive heart of mine—
As that we hear on Christmas morn
Upon the wintry breezes borne.

Though Darkness still her empire keep,
And hours must pass, ere morning break;
From troubled dreams, or slumbers deep,
That music *kindly* bids us wake:

It calls us, with an angel's voice,
To wake, and worship, and rejoice;

To greet with joy the glorious morn,
Which angels welcomed long ago,
When our redeeming Lord was born,
To bring the light of Heaven below;
The Powers of Darkness to dispel,
And rescue Earth from Death and Hell.

While listening to that sacred strain,
My raptured spirit soars on high
I seem to hear those songs again
Resounding through the open sky,
That kindled such divine delight,
In those who watched their flocks by night.

With them I celebrate His birth—
Glory to God in highest Heaven,
Good-will to men, and peace on earth,
To us a Saviour-king is given;
Our God is come to claim His own,
And Satan's power is overthrown!

A sinless God, for sinful men,
Descends to suffer and to bleed;
Hell *must* renounce its empire then;
The price is paid, the world is freed,
And Satan's self must now confess
That Christ has earned a *Right* to bless:

Now holy Peace may smile from Heaven,
And heavenly Truth from earth shall spring:
The captive's galling bonds are riven,
For our Redeemer is our king;
And He that gave His blood for men
Will lead us home to God again.

A CHRISTMAS TURKEY,
AND HOW IT CAME

Louisa May Alcott

"I know we couldn't do it."

"I say we could, if we all helped."

"How can we?"

"I've planned lots of ways; only you mustn't laugh at them, and you mustn't say a word to mother. I want it to be all a surprise."

"She'll find us out."

"No, she won't, if we tell her we won't get into mischief."

"Fire away, then, and let's hear your fine plans."

"We must talk softly, or we shall wake father. He's got a headache."

A curious change came over the faces of the two boys as their sister lowered her voice, with a nod toward a half-opened door. They looked sad and ashamed, and Kitty sighed as she spoke, for all knew that father's headaches always began by his coming home stupid or cross, with only a part of his wages; and mother always cried when she thought they did not see her, and after the long sleep father looked as if he didn't like to meet their eyes, but went off early.

They knew what it meant, but never spoke of it—only pondered over it, and mourned with mother at the change which was slowly altering their kind industrious father into a moody man, and mother into an anxious over-worked woman.

Kitty was thirteen, and a very capable girl, who helped with the housekeeping, took care of the two little ones, and went to school. Tommy and Sammy looked up to her and thought her a remarkably good sister. Now, as they sat round the stove having "a go-to-bed warm," the three heads were close together; and the boys listened eagerly to Kitty's plans, while the rattle of the sewing-machine in another room went on as tirelessly as it had done all day, for mother's work was more and more needed every month.

"Well!" began Kitty, in an impressive tone, "we all

know that there won't be a bit of Christmas in this family if we don't make it. Mother's too busy, and father don't care, so we must see what we can do; for I should be mortified to death to go to school and say I hadn't had any turkey or plum-pudding. Don't expect presents; but we must have some kind of a decent dinner."

"So I say; I'm tired of fish and potatoes," said Sammy, the younger.

"But where's the dinner coming from?" asked Tommy, who had already taken some of the cares of life on his young shoulders, and knew that Christmas dinners did not walk into people's houses without money.

"We'll earn it"; and Kitty looked like a small Napoleon planning the passage of the Alps. "You, Tom, must go early to-morrow to Mr. Brisket and offer to carry baskets. He will be dreadfully busy, and want you, I know; and you are so strong you can lug as much as some of the big fellows. He pays well, and if he won't give much money, you can take your wages in things to eat. We want everything."

"What shall I do?" cried Sammy, while Tom sat turning this plan over in his mind.

"Take the old shovel and clear sidewalks. The snow came on purpose to help you."

"It's awful hard work, and the shovel's half gone,"

began Sammy, who preferred to spend his holiday coasting on an old tea-tray.

"Don't growl, or you won't get any dinner," said Tom, making up his mind to lug baskets for the good of the family, like a manly lad as he was.

"I," continued Kitty, "have taken the hardest part of all; for after my work is done, and the babies safely settled, I'm going to beg for the leavings of the holly and pine swept out of the church down below, and make some wreaths and sell them."

"If you can," put in Tommy, who had tried pencils, and failed to make a fortune.

"Not in the street?" cried Sam, looking alarmed.

"Yes, at the corner of the Park. I'm bound to make some money, and don't see any other way. I shall put on an old hood and shawl, and no one will know me. Don't care if they do." And Kitty tried to mean what she said, but in her heart she felt that it would be a trial to her pride if any of her schoolmates should happen to recognize her.

"Don't believe you'll do it."

"See if I don't; for I will have a good dinner one day in the year."

"Well, it doesn't seem right for us to do it. Father ought to take care of us, and we only buy some presents with the little bit we earn. He never gives us anything now." And Tommy scowled at the bedroom door, with a strong sense of injury struggling with affection in his boyish heart.

"Hush!" cried Kitty. "Don't blame him. Mother says we never must forget he's our father. I try not to; but when she cries, it's hard to feel as I ought." And a sob made the little girl stop short as she poked the fire to hide the trouble in the face that should have been all smiles.

For a moment the room was very still, as the snow beat on the window, and the fire-light flickered over the six shabby little boots put up on the stove hearth to dry.

Tommy's cheerful voice broke the silence, saying stoutly, "Well, if I've got to work all day, I guess I'll go to bed early. Don't fret, Kit. We'll help all we can, and have a good time; see if we don't."

"I'll go out real early, and shovel like fury. Maybe I'll get a dollar. Would that buy a turkey?" asked Sammy, with the air of a millionaire.

"No, dear; one big enough for us would cost two, I'm afraid. Perhaps we'll have one sent us. We belong to the church, though folks don't know how poor we are now, and we can't beg." And Kitty bustled about, clearing up, rather exercised in her mind about going and asking for the much-desired fowl.

Soon all three were fast asleep, and nothing but the whir of the machine broke the quiet that fell upon the house. Then from the inner room a man came and sat over the fire with his head in his hands and his eyes fixed on the ragged little boots left to dry. He had heard the children's talk; and his heart was very heavy as he looked about the shabby room that used to be so neat and pleasant. What he thought no one knows, what he did we shall see by-and-by; but the sorrow and shame and tender silence of his children worked a miracle that night more lasting and lovely than the white beauty which the snow wrought upon the sleeping city.

Bright and early the boys were away to their work; while Kitty sang as she dressed the little sisters, put the house in order, and made her mother smile at the mysterious hints she gave of something splendid which was going to happen. Father was gone, and though all rather dreaded evening, nothing was said; but each worked with a will, feeling that Christmas should be merry in spite of poverty and care.

All day Tommy lugged fat turkeys, roasts of beef, and every sort of vegetable for other people's good dinners on the morrow, wondering meanwhile where his own was coming from. Mr. Brisket had an army of boys trudging here and there, and was too busy to notice any particular lad till the hurry was over, and only a few belated buyers remained to be served. It was late; but the stores kept open, and though so tired he could hardly stand, brave Tommy held on when the other boys left, hoping to earn a trifle more by extra work. He sat down on a barrel to rest during a leisure moment, and presently his weary head nodded sideways into a basket of cranberries, where he slept quietly till the sound of gruff voices roused him.

It was Mr. Brisket scolding because one dinner had been forgotten.

"I told that rascal Beals to be sure and carry it, for the old gentleman will be in a rage if it doesn't come, and take away his custom. Every boy gone, and I can't leave the store, nor you either, Pat, with all the clearing up to do."

"Here's a by, sir, slapin illigant forninst the cranberries, bad luck to him!" answered Pat, with a shake that set poor Tom on his legs, wide awake at once.

"Good luck to him, you mean. Here, What's-your-name, you take this basket to that number, and I'll make it worth your while," said Mr. Brisket, much relieved by this unexpected help.

"All right, sir"; and Tommy trudged off as briskly as his tired legs would let him, cheering the long cold walk with visions of the turkey with which his employer might reward

53

him, for there were piles of them, and Pat was to have one for his family.

His brilliant dreams were disappointed, however, for Mr. Brisket naturally supposed Tom's father would attend to that part of the dinner, and generously heaped a basket with vegetables, rosy apples, and a quart of cranberries.

"There, if you ain't too tired, you can take one more load to that number, and a merry Christmas to you!" said the stout man, handing over his gift with the promised dollar.

"Thank you, sir; good-night," answered Tom, shouldering his last load with a grateful smile, and trying not to look longingly at the poultry; for he had set his heart on at least a skinny bird as a surprise to Kit.

Sammy's adventures that day had been more varied and his efforts more successful, as we shall see, in the end, for Sammy was a most engaging little fellow, and no one could look into his blue eyes without wanting to pat his curly yellow head with one hand while the other gave him something. The cares of life had not lessened his confidence in people; and only the most abandoned ruffians had the heart to deceive or disappoint him. His very tribulations usually led to something pleasant, and whatever happened, sunshiny Sam came right side up, lucky and laughing.

Undaunted by the drifts or the cold wind, he marched off with the remains of the old shovel to seek his fortune, and found it at the third house where he called. The first two sidewalks were easy jobs; and he pocketed his nine-pences with a growing conviction that this was his chosen work. The third sidewalk was a fine long one, for the house stood on the corner, and two pavements must be cleared.

"It ought to be fifty cents; but perhaps they won't give me so much, I'm such a young one. I'll show 'em I can work, though, like a man"; and Sammy rang the bell with the energy of a telegraph boy.

Before the bell could be answered, a big boy rushed up, exclaiming roughly, "Get out of this! I'm going to have the job. You can't do it. Start, now, or I'll chuck you into a snow-bank."

"I won't!" answered Sammy, indignant at the brutal tone and unjust claim. "I got here first, and it's my job. You let me alone. I ain't afraid of you or your snow-banks either."

The big boy wasted no time in words, for steps were heard inside, but after a brief scuffle hauled Sammy, fighting bravely all the way, down the steps, and tumbled him into a deep drift. Then he ran up the steps, and respectfully asked for the job when a neat maid opened the door. He would have got it if Sam had not roared out, as he floundered in the drift, "I came first. He knocked me down 'cause I'm the smallest. Please let me do it; please!"

Before another word could be said, a little old lady appeared in the hall, trying to look stern, and failing entirely, because she was the picture of a dear fat, cosey grandma.

"Send that bad big boy away, Maria, and call in the poor little fellow. I saw the whole thing, and he shall have the job if he can do it."

The bully slunk away, and Sammy came panting up the steps, white with snow, a great bruise on his forehead, and a beaming smile on his face, looking so like a jolly little Santa Claus who had taken a "header" out of his sleigh that the maid laughed, and the old lady exclaimed, "Bless the boy! He's dreadfully hurt, and doesn't know it. Come in and be brushed and get your breath, child, and tell me how that scamp came to treat you so."

Nothing loath to be comforted, Sammy told his little tale while Maria dusted him off on the mat, and the old lady hovered in the doorway of the dining-room, where a nice breakfast smoked and smelled so deliciously that the boy sniffed the odor of coffee and buckwheats like a hungry hound.

"He'll get his death if he goes to work till he's dried a bit. Put him over the register, Maria, and I'll give him a hot drink, for it's bitter cold, poor dear!"

Away trotted the kind old lady, and in a minute came back with coffee and cakes, on which Sammy feasted as he warmed his toes and told Kitty's plans for Christmas, led on by the old lady's questions, and quite unconscious that he was letting all sorts of cats out of the bag.

Mrs. Bryant understood the little story, and made her plans also, for the rosy-faced boy was very like a little grandson who died last year, and her sad old heart was very tender to all other small boys. So she found out where Sammy lived, and nodded and smiled at him most cheerily as he tugged stoutly away at the snow on the long pavements till all was done, and the little workman came for his wages.

A bright silver dollar and a pocketful of gingerbread sent him off a rich and happy boy to shovel and sweep till noon, when he proudly showed his earnings at home, and feasted the babies on the carefully hoarded cake, for Dilly and Dot were the idols of the household.

"Now, Sammy dear, I want you to take my place here this afternoon, for mother will have to take her work home by-and-by, and I must sell my wreaths. I only got enough green for six, and two bunches of holly; but if

I can sell them for ten or twelve cents apiece, I shall be glad. Girls never can earn as much money as boys somehow," sighed Kitty, surveying the thin wreaths tied up with carpet ravellings, and vainly puzzling her young wits over a sad problem.

"I'll give you some of my money if you don't get a dollar; then we'll be even. Men always take care of women, you know, and ought to," cried Sammy, setting a fine example to his father, if he had only been there to profit by it.

With thanks Kitty left him to rest on the old sofa, while the happy babies swarmed over him; and putting on the shabby hood and shawl, she slipped away to stand at the Park gate, modestly offering her little wares to the passers-by. A nice old gentleman bought two, and his wife scolded him for getting such bad ones; but the money gave more happiness than any other he spent that day. A child took a ten-cent bunch of holly with its red berries, and there Kitty's market ended. It was very cold, people were in a hurry, bolder hucksters pressed before the timid little girl, and the balloon man told her to "clear out."

Hoping for better luck, she tried several other places; but the short afternoon was soon over, the streets began to thin, the keen wind chilled her to the bone, and her heart was very heavy to think that in all the rich, merry city, where

Christmas gifts passed her in every hand, there were none for the dear babies and boys at home, and the Christmas dinner was a failure.

"I must go and get supper anyway; and I'll hang these up in our own rooms, as I can't sell them," said Kitty, wiping a very big tear from her cold cheek, and turning to go away.

A smaller, shabbier girl than herself stood near, looking at the bunch of holly with wistful eyes; and glad to do to others as she wished someone would do to her, Kitty offered the only thing she had to give, saying kindly, "You may have it; merry Christmas!" and ran away before the delighted child could thank her.

I am very sure that one of the spirits who fly about at this season of the year saw the little act, made a note of it, and in about fifteen minutes rewarded Kitty for her sweet remembrance of the golden rule.

As she went sadly homeward she looked up at some of the big houses where every window shone with the festivities of Christmas Eve, and more than one tear fell, for the little girl found life pretty hard just then.

"There don't seem to be any wreaths at these windows; perhaps they'd buy mine. I can't bear to go home with so little for my share," she said, stopping before one of the biggest and brightest of these fairy palaces, where the sound of music was heard, and many little heads peeped from behind the curtains as if watching for some one.

Kitty was just going up the steps to make another trial, when two small boys came racing round the corner, slipped on the icy pavement, and both went down with a crash that would have broken older bones. One was up in a minute, laughing; the other lay squirming and howling, "Oh, my knee! my knee!" till Kitty ran and picked him up with the motherly consolations she had learned to give.

"It's broken; I know it is," wailed the small sufferer as Kitty carried him up the steps, while his friend wildly rang the doorbell.

It was like going into fairy-land, for the house was all astir with a children's Christmas party. Servants flew about with smiling faces; open doors gave ravishing glimpses of a feast in one room and a splendid tree in another; while a crowd of little faces peered over the balusters in the hall above, eager to come down and enjoy the glories prepared for them.

A pretty young girl came to meet Kitty, and listened to her story of the accident, which proved to be less severe than it at first appeared; for Bertie, the injured party, forgot his anguish at sight of the tree, and hopped upstairs so nimbly that every one laughed.

"He said his leg was broken, but I guess he's all right," said Kitty, reluctantly turning from this happy scene to go out into the night again.

"Would you like to see our tree before the children come down?" asked the pretty girl, seeing the wistful look in the child's eyes, and the shine of half-dried tears on her cheek.

"Oh, yes; I never saw anything so lovely. I'd like to tell the babies all about it"; and Kitty's face beamed at the prospect, as if the kind words had melted all the frost away.

"How many babies are there?" asked the pretty girl, as she led the way into the brilliant room. Kitty told her, adding several other facts, for the friendly atmosphere seemed to make them friends at once.

"I will buy the wreaths, for we haven't any," said the girl in silk, as Kitty told how she was just coming to offer them when the boys fell.

It was pretty to see how carefully the little hostess laid away the shabby garlands and slipped a half-dollar into Kitty's hand; prettier still, to watch the sly way in which she tucked some bonbons, a red ball, a blue whip, two china dolls, two pairs of little mittens, and some gilded nuts into an empty box for "the babies"; and prettiest of all, to see the smiles and tears make April in Kitty's face as she tried to tell her thanks for this beautiful surprise.

The world was all right when she got into the street again and ran home with the precious box hugged close, feeling that at last she had something to make a merry Christmas of.

Shrieks of joy greeted her, for Sammy's nice old lady had sent a basket full of pies, nuts and raisins, oranges and cake, and—oh, happy Sammy!—a sled, all for love of the blue eyes that twinkled so merrily when he told her about the tea-tray. Piled upon this red car of triumph, Dilly and Dot were being dragged about, while the other treasures were set forth on the table.

"I must show mine," cried Kitty; "we'll look at them to-night, and have them to-morrow"; and amid more cries of rapture her box was unpacked, her money added to the pile in the middle of the table, where Sammy had laid his handsome contribution toward the turkey.

Before the story of the splendid tree was over, in came Tommy with his substantial offering and his hard-earned dollar.

"I'm afraid I ought to keep my money for shoes. I've walked the soles off these to-day, and can't go to school barefooted," he said, bravely trying to put the temptation of skates behind him.

"We've got a good dinner without a turkey, and perhaps we'd better not get it," added Kitty, with a sigh, as she surveyed the table, and remembered the blue knit hood marked seventy-five cents that she saw in a shop-window.

"Oh, we must have a turkey! We worked so hard for it, and it's so Christmasy," cried Sam, who always felt that pleasant things ought to happen.

"Must have turty," echoed the babies, as they eyed the dolls tenderly.

"You shall have a turkey, and there he is," said an unexpected voice, as a noble bird fell upon the table, and lay there kicking up his legs as if enjoying the surprise immensely.

It was father's voice, and there stood father, neither cross nor stupid, but looking as he used to look, kind and happy, and beside him was mother, smiling as they had not seen her smile for months. It was not because the work was well paid for, and more promised, but because she had received a gift that made the world bright, a home happy again—father's promise to drink no more.

"I've been working to-day as well as you, and you may keep your money for yourselves. There are shoes for all; and never again, please God, shall my children be ashamed of me, or want a dinner Christmas Day."

As father said this with a choke in his voice, and mother's head went down on his shoulder to hide the happy tears that wet her cheeks, the children didn't know whether to laugh or cry, till Kitty, with the instinct of a loving heart, settled the question by saying, as she held out her hands, "We haven't any tree, so let's dance around our goodies and be merry."

Then the tired feet in the old shoes forgot their weariness, and five happy little souls skipped gayly round the table, where, in the midst of all the treasures earned and given, father's Christmas turkey proudly lay in state.

EPIPHANY

Christina Rossetti

"Lord Babe, if Thou art He

We sought for patiently,

Where is Thy court?

Hither may prophecy and star resort;

Men heed not their report."—

"Bow down and worship, righteous man:

This Infant of a span

Is He man sought for since the world began!"—

"Then, Lord, accept my gold, too base a thing

For Thee, of all kings King."—

"Lord Babe, despite Thy youth

I hold Thee of a truth
Both Good and Great:
But wherefore dost Thou keep so mean a state,
Low-lying desolate?"—
"Bow down and worship, righteous seer:
The Lord our God is here
Approachable, Who bids us all draw near."—
"Wherefore to Thee I offer frankincense,
Thou Sole Omnipotence."—

"But I have only brought
Myrrh; no wise afterthought
Instructed me
To gather pearls or gems, or choice to see
Coral or ivory."—
"Not least thine offering proves thee wise:
For myrrh means sacrifice,
And He that lives, this Same is He that dies."—
"Then here is myrrh: alas, yea woe is me
That myrrh befitteth Thee."—

Myrrh, frankincense, and gold:
And lo from wintry fold
Good-will doth bring

A Lamb, the innocent likeness of this King
Whom stars and seraphs sing:
And lo the bird of love, a Dove,
Flutters and coos above:
And Dove and Lamb and Babe agree in love:—
Come all mankind, come all creation hither,
Come, worship Christ together.

THE HOLY NIGHT

Elizabeth Barrett Browning

We sate among the stalls at Bethlehem;

The dumb kine from their fodder turning them,

Softened their horn'd faces,

To almost human gazes

Toward the newly Born:

The simple shepherds from the star-lit brooks

Brought visionary looks,

As yet in their astonished hearing rung

The strange sweet angel-tongue:

The magi of the East, in sandals worn,

Knelt reverent, sweeping round,

With long pale beards, their gifts upon the
    ground,
The incense, myrrh, and gold
These baby hands were impotent to hold:
So let all earthlies and celestials wait
Upon thy royal state.
Sleep, sleep, my kingly One!

THE GIFT OF THE MAGI

O. Henry

One dollar and eighty-seven cents. That was all. And sixty cents of it was in pennies. Pennies saved one and two at a time by bulldozing the grocer and the vegetable man and the butcher until one's cheeks burned with the silent imputation of parsimony that such close dealing implied. Three times Della counted it. One dollar and eighty-seven cents. And the next day would be Christmas.

There was clearly nothing to do but flop down on the shabby little couch and howl. So Della did it. Which instigates the moral reflection that life is made up of sobs, sniffles, and smiles, with sniffles predominating.

While the mistress of the home is gradually subsiding from the first stage to the second, take a look at the home. A furnished flat at $8 per week. It did not exactly beggar description, but it certainly had that word on the lookout for the mendicancy squad.

In the vestibule below was a letter-box into which no letter would go, and an electric button from which no mortal finger could coax a ring. Also appertaining thereunto was a card bearing the name "Mr. James Dillingham Young."

The "Dillingham" had been flung to the breeze during a former period of prosperity when its possessor was being paid $30 per week. Now, when the income was shrunk to $20, though, they were thinking seriously of contracting to a modest and unassuming D. But whenever Mr. James Dillingham Young came home and reached his flat above he was called "Jim" and greatly hugged by Mrs. James Dillingham Young, already introduced to you as Della. Which is all very good.

Della finished her cry and attended to her cheeks with the powder rag. She stood by the window and looked out dully at a gray cat walking a gray fence in a gray backyard. Tomorrow would be Christmas Day, and she had only $1.87 with which to buy Jim a present. She had been saving every penny she could for months, with this result. Twenty dollars a week doesn't go far. Expenses had been greater than she had calculated. They always are. Only $1.87 to buy a present for Jim. Her Jim. Many a happy hour she had spent planning for something nice for him. Something fine and rare and sterling—something just a little bit near to being worthy of the honor of being owned by Jim.

There was a pier glass between the windows of the room. Perhaps you have seen a pier glass in an $8 flat. A very thin and very agile person may, by observing his reflection in a rapid sequence of longitudinal strips, obtain a fairly accurate conception of his looks. Della, being slender, had mastered the art.

Suddenly she whirled from the window and stood before the glass. Her eyes were shining brilliantly, but her face had lost its color within twenty seconds. Rapidly she pulled down her hair and let it fall to its full length.

Now, there were two possessions of the James Dillingham Youngs in which they both took a mighty pride. One was Jim's gold watch that had been his father's and his grandfather's. The other was Della's hair. Had the queen of Sheba lived in the flat across the airshaft, Della would have let her hair hang out the window some day to dry just to depreciate Her Majesty's jewels and gifts. Had King Solomon been the janitor, with all his treasures piled up in the basement, Jim would have pulled out his watch every time he passed, just to see him pluck at his beard from envy.

So now Della's beautiful hair fell about her rippling and shining like a cascade of brown waters. It reached below her knee and made itself almost a garment for her. And then she did it up again nervously and quickly. Once she faltered for a minute and stood still while a tear or two splashed on the worn red carpet.

On went her old brown jacket; on went her old brown hat. With a whirl of skirts and with the brilliant sparkle still in her eyes, she fluttered out the door and down the stairs to the street.

Where she stopped the sign read: "Mme. Sofronie. Hair Goods of All Kinds." One flight up Della ran, and collected herself, panting. Madame, large, too white, chilly, hardly looked the "Sofronie."

"Will you buy my hair?" asked Della.

"I buy hair," said Madame. "Take yer hat off and let's have a sight at the looks of it."

Down rippled the brown cascade.

"Twenty dollars," said Madame, lifting the mass with a practiced hand.

"Give it to me quick," said Della.

Oh, and the next two hours tripped by on rosy wings.

Forget the hashed metaphor. She was ransacking the stores for Jim's present.

She found it at last. It surely had been made for Jim and no one else. There was no other like it in any of the stores, and she had turned all of them inside out. It was a platinum fob chain simple and chaste in design, properly proclaiming its value by substance alone and not by meretricious ornamentation—as all good things should do. It was even worthy of The Watch. As soon as she saw it she knew that it must be Jim's. It was like him. Quietness and value—the description applied to both. Twenty-one dollars they took from her for it, and she hurried home with the 87 cents. With that chain on his watch Jim might be properly anxious about the time in any company. Grand as the watch was, he sometimes looked at it on the sly on account of the old leather strap that he used in place of a chain.

When Della reached home her intoxication gave way a little to prudence and reason. She got out her curling irons and lighted the gas and went to work repairing the ravages made by generosity added to love. Which is always a tremendous task, dear friends—a mammoth task.

Within forty minutes her head was covered with tiny, close-lying curls that made her look wonderfully like a truant schoolboy. She looked at her reflection in the mirror long, carefully, and critically.

"If Jim doesn't kill me," she said to herself, "before he takes a second look at me, he'll say I look like a Coney Island chorus girl. But what could I do—oh! what could I do with a dollar and eighty-seven cents?"

At seven o'clock the coffee was made and the frying pan was on the back of the stove hot and ready to cook the chops.

Jim was never late. Della doubled the fob chain in her hand and sat on the corner of the table near the door that he always entered. Then she heard his step on the stair away down on the first flight, and she turned white for just a moment. She had a habit of saying a little silent prayer about the simplest everyday things, and now she whispered: "Please God, make him think I am still pretty."

The door opened and Jim stepped in and closed it. He looked thin and very serious. Poor fellow, he was only twenty-two—and to be burdened with a family! He needed a new overcoat and he was without gloves.

Jim stopped inside the door, as immovable as a setter at the scent of quail. His eyes were fixed upon Della, and there was an expression in them that she could not read, and it terrified her. It was not anger, nor surprise, nor disapproval, nor horror, nor any of the sentiments that she had been prepared for. He simply stared at her fixedly with that peculiar expression on his face.

Della wriggled off the table and went for him.

"Jim, darling," she cried, "don't look at me that way. I had my hair cut off and sold because I couldn't have lived through Christmas without giving you a present. It'll grow out again—you won't mind, will you? I just had to do it. My hair grows awfully fast. Say 'Merry Christmas!' Jim, and let's be happy. You don't know what a nice—what a beautiful, nice gift I've got for you."

"You've cut off your hair?" asked Jim, laboriously, as if he had not arrived at that patent fact yet even after the hardest mental labor.

"Cut it off and sold it," said Della. "Don't you like me just as well, anyhow? I'm me without my hair, ain't I?"

Jim looked about the room curiously.

"You say your hair is gone?" he said, with an air almost of idiocy.

"You needn't look for it," said Della. "It's sold, I tell you—sold and gone, too. It's Christmas Eve, boy. Be good to me, for it went for you. Maybe the hairs of my head were numbered," she went on with sudden serious sweetness, "but nobody could ever count my love for you. Shall I put the chops on, Jim?"

Out of his trance Jim seemed quickly to wake. He enfolded his Della. For ten seconds let us regard with discreet scrutiny some inconsequential object in the other direction. Eight dollars a week or a million a year—what is the difference? A mathematician or a wit would give you the wrong answer. The magi brought valuable gifts, but that was not among them. This dark assertion will be illuminated later on.

Jim drew a package from his overcoat pocket and threw it upon the table.

"Don't make any mistake, Dell," he said, "about me. I don't think there's anything in the way of a haircut or a shave or a shampoo that could make me like my girl any less. But if you'll unwrap that package you may see why you had me going a while at first."

White fingers and nimble tore at the string and paper. And then an ecstatic scream of joy; and then, alas! a quick feminine change to hysterical tears and wails, necessitating the immediate employment of all the comforting powers of the lord of the flat.

For there lay The Combs—the set of combs, side and back, that Della had worshipped long in a Broadway window. Beautiful combs, pure tortoise shell, with jewelled rims—just the shade to wear in the beautiful vanished hair.

They were expensive combs, she knew, and her heart had simply craved and yearned over them without the least hope of possession. And now, they were hers, but the tresses that should have adorned the coveted adornments were gone.

But she hugged them to her bosom, and at length she was able to look up with dim eyes and a smile and say: "My hair grows so fast, Jim!"

And then Della leaped up like a little singed cat and cried, "Oh, oh!"

Jim had not yet seen his beautiful present. She held it out to him eagerly upon her open palm. The dull precious metal seemed to flash with a reflection of her bright and ardent spirit.

"Isn't it a dandy, Jim? I hunted all over town to find it. You'll have to look at the time a hundred times a day now. Give me your watch. I want to see how it looks on it."

Instead of obeying, Jim tumbled down on the couch and put his hands under the back of his head and smiled.

"Dell," said he, "let's put our Christmas presents away and keep 'em a while. They're too nice to use just at present. I sold the watch to get the money to buy your combs. And now suppose you put the chops on."

The magi, as you know, were wise men—wonderfully wise men—who brought gifts to the Babe in the manger.

They invented the art of giving Christmas presents. Being wise, their gifts were no doubt wise ones, possibly bearing the privilege of exchange in case of duplication. And here I have lamely related to you the uneventful chronicle of two foolish children in a flat who most unwisely sacrificed for each other the greatest treasures of their house. But in a last word to the wise of these days let it be said that of all who give gifts these two were the wisest. Of all who give and receive gifts, such as they are wisest. Everywhere they are wisest. They are the magi.

CHRISTMAS BELLS

Henry Wadsworth Longfellow

I heard the bells on Christmas Day

Their old, familiar carols play,

    And wild and sweet

    The words repeat

Of peace on earth, good-will to men!

And thought how, as the day had come,

The belfries of all Christendom

    Had rolled along

    The unbroken song

Of peace on earth, good-will to men!

Till ringing, singing on its way,
The world revolved from night to day,
     A voice, a chime,
     A chant sublime
Of peace on earth, good-will to men!

Then from each black, accursed mouth
The cannon thundered in the South,
     And with the sound
     The carols drowned
Of peace on earth, good-will to men!

It was as if an earthquake rent
The hearth-stones of a continent,
     And made forlorn
     The households born
Of peace on earth, good-will to men!

And in despair I bowed my head;
"There is no peace on earth," I said;
     "For hate is strong,
     And mocks the song
Of peace on earth, good-will to men!"

Then pealed the bells more loud and deep:
"God is not dead, nor doth He sleep;
    The Wrong shall fail,
    The Right prevail,
With peace on earth, good-will to men."

A Christmas Carol

Christina Rossetti

In the bleak mid-winter
    Frosty wind made moan,
Earth stood hard as iron,
    Water like a stone;
Snow had fallen, snow on snow,
    Snow on snow,
In the bleak mid-winter
    Long ago.

Our God, Heaven cannot hold Him
    Nor earth sustain;
Heaven and earth shall flee away

When He comes to reign:
In the bleak midwinter
    A stable-place sufficed
The Lord God Almighty
    Jesus Christ.

Enough for Him, whom cherubim
    Worship night and day,
A breastful of milk
    And a mangerful of hay;
Enough for Him, whom angels
    Fall down before,
The ox and ass and camel
    Which adore.

Angels and archangels
    May have gathered there,
Cherubim and seraphim
    Thronged the air;
But only His mother
    In her maiden bliss
Worshipped the Beloved
    With a kiss.

What can I give Him,
      Poor as I am?
If I were a shepherd
      I would bring a lamb,
If I were a Wise Man
      I would do my part,—
Yet what I can I give Him,
      Give my heart.

CHRISTMAS AT RED BUTTE

L. M. Montgomery

"Of course Santa Claus will come," said Jimmy Martin confidently. Jimmy was ten, and at ten it is easy to be confident. "Why, he's *got* to come because it is Christmas Eve, and he always *has* come. You know that, twins."

Yes, the twins knew it and, cheered by Jimmy's superior wisdom, their doubts passed away. There had been one terrible moment when Theodora had sighed and told them they mustn't be too much disappointed if Santa Claus did not come this year because the crops had been poor, and he mightn't have had enough presents to go around.

"That doesn't make any difference to Santa Claus," scoffed Jimmy. "You know as well as I do, Theodora

Prentice, that Santa Claus is rich whether the crops fail or not. They failed three years ago, before Father died, but Santa Claus came all the same. Prob'bly you don't remember it, twins, 'cause you were too little, but I do. Of course he'll come, so don't you worry a mite. And he'll bring my skates and your dolls. He knows we're expecting them, Theodora, 'cause we wrote him a letter last week, and threw it up the chimney. And there'll be candy and nuts, of course, and Mother's gone to town to buy a turkey. I tell you we're going to have a ripping Christmas."

"Well, don't use such slangy words about it, Jimmy-boy," sighed Theodora. She couldn't bear to dampen their hopes any further, and perhaps Aunt Elizabeth might manage it if the colt sold well. But Theodora had her painful doubts, and she sighed again as she looked out of the window far down the trail that wound across the prairie, red-lighted by the declining sun of the short wintry afternoon.

"Do people always sigh like that when they get to be sixteen?" asked Jimmy curiously. "You didn't sigh like that when you were only fifteen, Theodora. I wish you wouldn't. It makes me feel funny—and it's not a nice kind of funniness either."

"It's a bad habit I've got into lately," said Theodora, trying to laugh. "Old folks are dull sometimes, you know, Jimmy-boy."

"Sixteen is awful old, isn't it?" said Jimmy reflectively. "I'll tell you what I'm going to do when I'm sixteen, Theodora. I'm going to pay off the mortgage, and buy mother a silk dress, and a piano for the twins. Won't that be elegant? I'll be able to do that 'cause I'm a man. Of course if I was only a girl I couldn't."

"I hope you'll be a good kind brave man and a real help to your mother," said Theodora softly, sitting down before the cosy fire and lifting the fat little twins into her lap.

"Oh, I'll be good to her, never you fear," assured Jimmy, squatting comfortably down on the little fur rug before the stove—the skin of the coyote his father had killed four years ago. "I believe in being good to your mother when you've only got the one. Now tell us a story, Theodora—a real jolly story, you know, with lots of fighting in it. Only please don't kill anybody. I like to hear about fighting, but I like to have all the people come out alive."

Theodora laughed, and began a story about the Riel Rebellion of '85—a story which had the double merit of being true and exciting at the same time. It was quite dark when she finished, and the twins were nodding, but Jimmy's eyes were wide open and sparkling.

"That was great," he said, drawing a long breath. "Tell us another."

"No, it's bedtime for you all," said Theodora firmly. "One story at a time is my rule, you know."

"But I want to sit up till Mother comes home," objected Jimmy.

"You can't. She may be very late, for she would have to wait to see Mr. Porter. Besides, you don't know what time Santa Claus might come—if he comes at all. If he were to drive along and see you children up instead of being sound asleep in bed, he might go right on and never call at all."

This argument was too much for Jimmy.

"All right, we'll go. But we have to hang up our stockings first. Twins, get yours."

The twins toddled off in great excitement, and brought back their Sunday stockings, which Jimmy proceeded to hang along the edge of the mantel shelf. This done, they all trooped obediently off to bed. Theodora gave another sigh, and seated herself at the window, where she could watch the moonlit prairie for Mrs. Martin's homecoming and knit at the same time.

I am afraid that you will think from all the sighing Theodora was doing that she was a very melancholy and despondent young lady. You couldn't think anything more unlike the real Theodora. She was the jolliest, bravest girl of sixteen in all Saskatchewan, as her shining brown eyes and rosy, dimpled cheeks would have told you; and her sighs were not on her own account, but simply for fear the children were going to be disappointed. She knew that they would be almost heartbroken if Santa Claus did not come, and that this would hurt the patient hardworking little mother more than all else.

Five years before this, Theodora had come to live with Uncle George and Aunt Elizabeth in the little log house at Red Butte. Her own mother had just died, and Theodora had only her big brother Donald left, and Donald had Klondike fever. The Martins were poor, but they had gladly made room for their little niece, and Theodora had lived there ever since, her aunt's right-hand girl and the beloved playmate of the children. They had been very happy until Uncle George's death two years before this Christmas Eve; but since then there had been hard times in the little log house, and though Mrs. Martin and Theodora did their best, it was a woefully hard task to make both ends meet, especially this year when their crops had been poor. Theodora and her aunt had made every sacrifice possible for the children's sake, and at least Jimmy and the twins had not felt the pinch very severely yet.

At seven Mrs. Martin's bells jingled at the door and Theodora flew out. "Go right in and get warm, Auntie," she said briskly. "I'll take Ned away and unharness him."

"It's a bitterly cold night," said Mrs. Martin wearily. There was a note of discouragement in her voice that struck dismay to Theodora's heart.

"I'm afraid it means no Christmas for the children tomorrow," she thought sadly, as she led Ned away to the stable. When she returned to the kitchen Mrs. Martin was sitting by the fire, her face in her chilled hand, sobbing convulsively.

"Auntie—oh, Auntie, don't!" exclaimed Theodora impulsively. It was such a rare thing to see her plucky, resolute little aunt in tears. "You're cold and tired—I'll have a nice cup of tea for you in a trice."

"No, it isn't that," said Mrs. Martin brokenly. "It was seeing those stockings hanging there. Theodora, I couldn't get a thing for the children—not a single thing. Mr. Porter would only give forty dollars for the colt, and when all the bills were paid there was barely enough left for such necessaries as we must have. I suppose I ought to feel thankful I could get those. But the thought of the children's disappointment tomorrow is more than I can bear. It would have been better to have told them long ago, but I kept building on getting more for the colt. Well, it's weak and foolish to give way like this. We'd better both take a cup of tea and go to bed. It will save fuel."

When Theodora went up to her little room her face was very thoughtful. She took a small box from her table and carried it to the window. In it was a very pretty little gold locket hung on a narrow blue ribbon. Theodora held it tenderly in her fingers, and looked out over the moonlit prairie with a very sober face. Could she give up her dear locket—the locket Donald had given her just before he started for the Klondike? She had never thought she could do such a thing. It was almost the only thing she had to remind her of Donald—handsome, merry, impulsive, warmhearted Donald, who had gone away four years ago with a smile on his bonny face and splendid hope in his heart.

"Here's a locket for you, Gift o' God," he had said gaily—he had such a dear loving habit of calling her by the beautiful meaning of her name. A lump came into Theodora's throat as she remembered it. "I couldn't afford a chain too, but when I come back I'll bring you a rope of Klondike nuggets for it."

Then he had gone away. For two years letters had come from him regularly. Then he wrote that he had joined a prospecting party to a remote wilderness. After that was silence, deepening into anguish of suspense that finally ended in hopelessness. A rumour came that Donald Prentice was dead. None had returned from the expedition he had joined. Theodora had long ago given up all hope of ever seeing Donald again. Hence her locket was doubly dear to her.

But Aunt Elizabeth had always been so good and loving and kind to her. Could she not make the sacrifice for her sake? Yes, she could and would. Theodora flung up her head with a gesture that meant decision. She took out of the locket the bits of hair—her mother's and Donald's—which it contained (perhaps a tear or two fell as she did so) and then hastily donned her warmest cap and wraps. It was only three miles to Spencer; she could easily walk it in an hour and, as it was Christmas Eve, the shops would be open late. She must walk, for Ned could not be taken out again, and the mare's foot was sore. Besides, Aunt Elizabeth must not know until it was done.

As stealthily as if she were bound on some nefarious errand, Theodora slipped downstairs and out of the house. The next minute she was hurrying along the trail in the moonlight. The great dazzling prairie was around her, the mystery and splendour of the northern night all about her. It was very calm and cold, but Theodora walked so briskly that she kept warm. The trail from Red Butte to Spencer was a lonely one. Mr. Lurgan's house, halfway to town, was the only dwelling on it.

When Theodora reached Spencer she made her way at once to the only jewellery store the little town contained. Mr. Benson, its owner, had been a friend of her uncle's, and Theodora felt sure that he would buy her locket. Nevertheless her heart beat quickly, and her breath came and went uncomfortably fast as she went in. Suppose he wouldn't buy it. Then there would be no Christmas for the children at Red Butte.

"Good evening, Miss Theodora," said Mr. Benson briskly. "What can I do for you?"

"I'm afraid I'm not a very welcome sort of customer, Mr. Benson," said Theodora, with an uncertain smile. "I want to sell, not buy. Could you—will you buy this locket?"

Mr. Benson pursed up his lips, took up the locket, and examined it. "Well, I don't often buy second-hand stuff," he said, after some reflection, "but I don't mind obliging you, Miss Theodora. I'll give you four dollars for this trinket."

Theodora knew the locket had cost a great deal more than that, but four dollars would get what she wanted, and she dared not ask for more. In a few minutes the locket was in Mr. Benson's possession, and Theodora, with four crisp new bills in her purse, was hurrying to the toy store. Half an hour later she was on her way back to Red Butte, with as many parcels as she could carry—Jimmy's skates, two lovely dolls for the twins, packages of nuts and candy, and a nice plump turkey. Theodora beguiled her lonely tramp by picturing the children's joy in the morning.

About a quarter of a mile past Mr. Lurgan's house the trail curved suddenly about a bluff of poplars. As Theodora rounded the turn she halted in amazement. Almost at her feet the body of a man was lying across the road. He was clad in a big fur coat, and had a fur cap pulled well down over his forehead and ears. Almost all of him that could be seen was a full bushy beard. Theodora had no idea who he was, or where he had come from. But she realized that he was unconscious, and that he would speedily freeze to death if help were not brought. The footprints of a horse galloping across the prairie suggested a fall and a runaway, but Theodora did not waste time in speculation. She ran back at full speed to Mr. Lurgan's, and roused the household. In a few minutes Mr. Lurgan and his son had hitched a horse to a wood-sleigh, and hurried down the trail to the unfortunate man.

Theodora, knowing that her assistance was not needed, and that she ought to get home as quickly as possible, went on her way as soon as she had seen the stranger in safe keeping. When she reached the little log house she crept in, cautiously put the children's gifts in their stockings, placed the turkey on the table where Aunt Elizabeth would see it the first thing in the morning, and then slipped off to bed, a very weary but very happy girl.

The joy that reigned in the little log house the next day more than repaid Theodora for her sacrifice.

"Whoopee, didn't I tell you that Santa Claus would come all right!" shouted the delighted Jimmy. "Oh, what splendid skates!"

The twins hugged their dolls in silent rapture, but Aunt Elizabeth's face was the best of all.

Then the dinner had to be prepared, and everybody had a hand in that. Just as Theodora, after a grave peep into the oven, had announced that the turkey was done, a sleigh dashed around the house. Theodora flew to answer the knock at the door, and there stood Mr. Lurgan and a big, bewhiskered, fur-coated fellow whom Theodora recognized as the stranger she had found on the trail. But—was he a stranger? There was something oddly familiar in those merry brown eyes. Theodora felt herself growing dizzy.

"Donald!" she gasped. "Oh, Donald!"

And then she was in the big fellow's arms, laughing and crying at the same time.

Donald it was indeed. And then followed half an hour during which everybody talked at once, and the turkey would have been burned to a crisp had it not been for the presence of mind of Mr. Lurgan who, being the least excited of them all, took it out of the oven, and set it on the back of the stove.

"To think that it was you last night, and that I never dreamed it," exclaimed Theodora. "Oh, Donald, if I hadn't gone to town!"

"I'd have frozen to death, I'm afraid," said Donald soberly. "I got into Spencer on the last train last night. I felt that I must come right out—I couldn't wait till morning. But there wasn't a team to be got for love or money—it was Christmas Eve and all the livery rigs were out. So I came on horseback. Just by that bluff something frightened my horse, and he shied violently. I was half asleep and thinking of my little sister, and I went off like a shot. I suppose I struck my head against a tree. Anyway, I knew nothing more until I came to in Mr. Lurgan's kitchen. I wasn't much hurt—feel none the worse of it except for a sore head and shoulder. But, oh, Gift o' God, how you have grown! I can't realize that you are the little sister I left four years ago. I suppose you have been thinking I was dead?"

"Yes, and, oh, Donald, where have you been?"

"Well, I went way up north with a prospecting party. We had a tough time the first year, I can tell you, and some of us never came back. We weren't in a country where post offices were lying round loose either, you see. Then at last, just as we were about giving up in despair, we struck it rich. I've brought a snug little pile home with me, and things are going to look up in this log house, Gift o' God. There'll be no more worrying for you dear people over mortgages."

"I'm so glad—for Auntie's sake," said Theodora, with shining eyes. "But, oh, Donald, it's best of all just to have you back. I'm so perfectly happy that I don't know what to do or say."

"Well, I think you might have dinner," said Jimmy in an injured tone. "The turkey's getting stone cold, and I'm most starving. I just can't stand it another minute."

So, with a laugh, they all sat down to the table and ate the merriest Christmas dinner the little log house had ever known.

THE WAITS

Margaret Deland

At the break of Christmas Day,

    Through the frosty starlight ringing,

Faint and sweet and far away,

    Comes the sound of children, singing,

        Chanting, singing,

     "Cease to mourn,

     For Christ is born,

       Peace and joy to all men bringing!"

Careless that the chill winds blow,

    Growing stronger, sweeter, clearer,

Noiseless footfalls in the snow,

Bring the happy voices nearer;
 Hear them singing,
"Winter's drear,
But Christ is here,
 Mirth and gladness with Him bringing."

"Merry Christmas!" hear them say,
 As the East is growing lighter;
"May the joy of Christmas Day
 Make your whole year gladder, brighter!"
  Join their singing,
"To each home
Our Christ has come,
 All Love's treasures with Him bringing!"

CHRISTMAS IN THE HEART

Paul Laurence Dunbar

The snow lies deep upon the ground,

And winter's brightness all around

Decks bravely out the forest sere,

With jewels of the brave old year.

The coasting crowd upon the hill

With some new spirit seems to thrill;

And all the temple bells achime.

Ring out the glee of Christmas time.

In happy homes the brown oak-bough

Vies with the red-gemmed holly now;

And here and there, like pearls, there show

The berries of the mistletoe.

A sprig upon the chandelier

Says to the maidens, "Come not here!"

Even the pauper of the earth

Some kindly gift has cheered to mirth!

Within his chamber, dim and cold,

There sits a grasping miser old.

He has no thought save one of gain,—

To grind and gather and grasp and drain.

A peal of bells, a merry shout

Assail his ear: he gazes out

Upon a world to him all gray,

And snarls, "Why, this is Christmas Day!"

No, man of ice,—for shame, for shame!

For "Christmas Day" is no mere name.

No, not for you this ringing cheer,

This festal season of the year.

And not for you the chime of bells

From holy temple rolls and swells.

In day and deed he has no part—

Who holds not Christmas in his heart!

THE FIR TREE

Hans Christian Andersen

Far away in the forest, where the warm sun and the fresh air made a sweet resting place, grew a pretty little fir tree. The situation was all that could be desired; and yet the tree was not happy, it wished so much to be like its tall companions, the pines and firs which grew around it.

The sun shone, and the soft air fluttered its leaves, and the little peasant children passed by, prattling merrily; but the fir tree did not heed them.

Sometimes the children would bring a large basket of raspberries or strawberries, wreathed on straws, and seat themselves near the fir tree, and say, "Is it not a pretty little tree?" which made it feel even more unhappy than before.

And yet all this while the tree grew a notch or joint taller every year, for by the number of joints in the stem of a fir tree we can discover its age.

Still, as it grew, it complained: "Oh! how I wish I were as tall as the other trees; then I would spread out my branches on every side, and my crown would overlook the wide world around. I should have the birds building their nests on my boughs, and when the wind blew, I should bow with stately dignity, like my tall companions."

So discontented was the tree, that it took no pleasure in the warm sunshine, the birds, or the rosy clouds that floated over it morning and evening.

Sometimes in winter, when the snow lay white and glittering on the ground, there was a little hare that would come springing along, and jump right over the little tree's head; then how mortified it would feel.

Two winters passed; and when the third arrived, the tree had grown so tall that the hare was obliged to run round it. Yet it remained unsatisfied and would exclaim: "Oh! to grow, to grow; if I could but keep on growing tall and old! There is nothing else worth caring for in the world."

In the autumn the woodcutters came, as usual, and cut down several of the tallest trees; and the young fir, which was now grown to a good, full height, shuddered as the noble trees fell to the earth with a crash.

After the branches were lopped off, the trunks looked so slender and bare that they could scarcely be recognized. Then they were placed, one upon another, upon wagons and drawn by horses out of the forest. Where could they be going? What would become of them? The young fir tree wished very much to know.

So in the spring, when the swallows and the storks came, it asked: "Do you know where those trees were taken? Did you meet them?"

The swallows knew nothing; but the stork, after a little reflection, nodded his head and said: "Yes, I think I do. As I flew from Egypt, I met several new ships, and they had fine masts that smelt like fir. These must have been the trees; and I assure you they were stately; they sailed right gloriously!"

"Oh, how I wish I were tall enough to go on the sea," said the fir tree. "Tell me what is this sea, and what does it look like?"

"It would take too much time to explain—a great deal too much," said the stork, flying quickly away.

"Rejoice in thy youth," said the sunbeam; "rejoice in thy fresh growth and in the young life that is in thee."

And the wind kissed the tree, and the dew watered it with tears, but the fir tree regarded them not.

Christmas time drew near, and many young trees were cut down, some that were even smaller and younger than the fir tree, who enjoyed neither rest nor peace for longing to leave its forest home. These young trees, which were chosen for their beauty, kept their branches, and they, also, were laid on wagons and drawn by horses far away out of the forest.

"Where are they going?" asked the fir tree. "They are not taller than I am; indeed, one is not so tall. And why do they keep all their branches? Where are they going?"

"We know, we know," sang the sparrows; "we have looked in at the windows of the houses in the town, and we know what is done with them. Oh! you cannot think what honor and glory they receive. They are dressed up in the most splendid manner. We have seen them standing in the middle of a warm room, and adorned with all sorts of beautiful things—honey cakes, gilded apples, playthings, and many hundreds of wax tapers."

"And then," asked the fir tree, trembling in all its branches, "and then what happens?"

"We did not see any more," said the sparrows; "but this was enough for us."

"I wonder whether anything so brilliant will ever happen to me," thought the fir tree. "It would be better even than crossing the sea. I long for it almost with pain. Oh, when will Christmas be here? I am now as tall and well grown as those which were taken away last year. O that I were now laid on the wagon, or standing in the warm room with all that brightness and splendor around me! Something better and more beautiful is to come after, or the trees would not be so decked out. Yes, what follows will be grander and more splendid. What can it be? I am weary with longing. I scarcely know what it is that I feel."

"Rejoice in our love," said the air and the sunlight. "Enjoy thine own bright life in the fresh air."

But the tree would not rejoice, though it grew taller every day, and winter and summer its dark-green foliage might be seen in the forest, while passers-by would say, "What a beautiful tree!"

A short time before the next Christmas the discontented fir tree was the first to fall. As the ax cut sharply through the stem and divided the pith, the tree fell with a groan to the earth, conscious of pain and faintness and forgetting all its dreams of happiness in sorrow at leaving its home in the forest. It knew that it should never again see its dear old companions the trees, nor the little bushes and many-colored flowers that had grown by its side; perhaps not even the birds. Nor was the journey at all pleasant.

The tree first recovered itself while being unpacked in the courtyard of a house, with several other trees; and it heard a man say: "We only want one, and this is the prettiest. This is beautiful!"

Then came two servants in grand livery and carried the fir tree into a large and beautiful apartment. Pictures hung on the walls, and near the tall tile stove stood great china vases with lions on the lids. There were rocking-chairs, silken sofas, and large tables covered with pictures; and there were books, and playthings that had cost a hundred times a hundred dollars—at least so said the children.

Then the fir tree was placed in a large tub full of sand— but green baize hung all round it so that no one could know it was a tub—and it stood on a very handsome carpet. Oh, how the fir tree trembled! What was going to happen to him now? Some young ladies came, and the servants helped them to adorn the tree.

On one branch they hung little bags cut out of colored paper, and each bag was filled with sweetmeats. From other branches hung gilded apples and walnuts, as if they had grown there; and above and all around were hundreds of red, blue, and white tapers, which were fastened upon the branches. Dolls, exactly like real men and women, were placed under the green leaves—the tree had never seen such things before—and at the very top was fastened a glittering star made of gold tinsel. Oh, it was very beautiful. "This evening," they all exclaimed, "how bright it will be!"

"O that the evening were come," thought the tree, "and the tapers lighted! Then I shall know what else is going to happen. Will the trees of the forest come to see me? Will the sparrows peep in at the windows, I wonder, as they fly? Shall I grow faster here than in the forest, and shall I keep on all these ornaments during summer and winter?" But guessing was of very little use. His back ached with trying, and this pain is as bad for a slender fir tree as headache is for us.

At last the tapers were lighted, and then what a glistening blaze of splendor the tree presented! It trembled so with joy in all its branches that one of the candles fell among the green leaves and burned some of them. "Help! help!" exclaimed the young ladies; but no harm was done, for they quickly extinguished the fire.

After this the tree tried not to tremble at all, though

the fire frightened him, he was so anxious not to hurt any of the beautiful ornaments, even while their brilliancy dazzled him.

And now the folding doors were thrown open, and a troop of children rushed in as if they intended to upset the tree, and were followed more slowly by their elders. For a moment the little ones stood silent with astonishment, and then they shouted for joy till the room rang; and they danced merrily round the tree while one present after another was taken from it.

"What are they doing? What will happen next?" thought the tree. At last the candles burned down to the branches and were put out. Then the children received permission to plunder the tree.

Oh, how they rushed upon it! There was such a riot that the branches cracked, and had it not been fastened with the glistening star to the ceiling, it must have been thrown down.

Then the children danced about with their pretty toys, and no one noticed the tree except the children's maid, who came and peeped among the branches to see if an apple or a fig had been forgotten.

"A story, a story," cried the children, pulling a little fat man towards the tree.

"Now we shall be in the green shade," said the man as he seated himself under it, "and the tree will have the pleasure of hearing, also; but I shall only relate one story. What shall it be? Ivede-Avede or Humpty Dumpty, who fell downstairs, but soon got up again, and at last married a princess?"

"Ivede-Avede," cried some; "Humpty Dumpty," cried others; and there was a famous uproar. But the fir tree remained quite still and thought to himself: "Shall I have anything to do with all this? Ought I to make a noise, too?" but he had already amused them as much as they wished and they paid no attention to him.

Then the old man told them the story of Humpty Dumpty—how he fell downstairs, and was raised up again, and married a princess. And the children clapped their hands and cried, "Tell another, tell another," for they wanted to hear the story of Ivede-Avede; but this time they had only "Humpty Dumpty." After this the fir tree became quite silent and thoughtful. Never had the birds in the forest told such tales as that of Humpty Dumpty, who fell downstairs, and yet married a princess.

"Ah, yes! so it happens in the world," thought the fir tree. He believed it all, because it was related by such a pleasant man.

"Ah, well!" he thought, "who knows? Perhaps I may fall down, too, and marry a princess"; and he looked forward joyfully to the next evening, expecting to be again decked out with lights and playthings, gold and fruit. "To-morrow I will not tremble," thought he; "I will enjoy all my splendor, and I shall hear the story of Humpty Dumpty again, and perhaps of Ivede-Avede." And the tree remained quiet and thoughtful all night.

In the morning the servants and the housemaid came in. "Now," thought the fir tree, "all my splendor is going to begin again." But they dragged him out of the room and upstairs to the garret and threw him on the floor in a dark corner where no daylight shone, and there they left him. "What does this mean?" thought the tree. "What am I to do here? I can hear nothing in a place like this;" and he leaned against the wall and thought and thought.

And he had time enough to think, for days and nights passed and no one came near him; and when at last somebody did come, it was only to push away some large boxes in a corner. So the tree was completely hidden from sight, as if it had never existed.

"It is winter now," thought the tree; "the ground is hard and covered with snow, so that people cannot plant me. I shall be sheltered here, I dare say, until spring comes. How thoughtful and kind everybody is to me! Still, I wish this place were not so dark and so dreadfully lonely, with not even a little hare to look at. How pleasant it was out in the forest while the snow lay on the ground, when the hare would run by, yes, and jump over me, too, although I did not like it then. Oh! it is terribly lonely here."

"Squeak, squeak," said a little mouse, creeping cautiously towards the tree; then came another, and they both sniffed at the fir tree and crept in and out between the branches.

"Oh, it is very cold," said the little mouse. "If it were not we should be very comfortable here, shouldn't we, old fir tree?"

"I am not old," said the fir tree. "There are many who are older than I am."

"Where do you come from?" asked the mice, who were full of curiosity; "and what do you know? Have you seen the most beautiful places in the world, and can you tell us all about them? And have you been in the storeroom, where cheeses lie on the shelf and hams hang from the ceiling? One can run about on tallow candles there; one can go in thin and come out fat."

"I know nothing of that," said the fir tree, "but I know the wood, where the sun shines and the birds sing." And then the tree told the little mice all about its youth. They had never heard such an account in their lives; and after they had listened to it attentively, they said: "What a number of things you have seen! You must have been very happy."

"Happy!" exclaimed the fir tree; and then, as he reflected on what he had been telling them, he said, "Ah, yes! after all, those were happy days." But when he went on and related all about Christmas Eve, and how he had been dressed up with cakes and lights, the mice said, "How happy you must have been, you old fir tree."

"I am not old at all," replied the tree; "I only came from the forest this winter. I am now checked in my growth."

"What splendid stories you can tell," said the little mice. And the next night four other mice came with them to hear what the tree had to tell. The more he talked the more he remembered, and then he thought to himself: "Yes, those were happy days; but they may come again. Humpty Dumpty fell downstairs, and yet he married the princess. Perhaps I may marry a princess, too." And the fir tree thought of the pretty little birch tree that grew in the forest; a real princess, a beautiful princess, she was to him.

"Who is Humpty Dumpty?" asked the little mice. And then the tree related the whole story; he could remember every single word. And the little mice were so delighted with it that they were ready to jump to the top of the tree. The next night a great many more mice made their appearance, and on Sunday two rats came with them; but the rats said it was not a pretty story at all, and the little mice were very sorry, for it made them also think less of it.

"Do you know only that one story?" asked the rats.

"Only that one," replied the fir tree. "I heard it on the happiest evening in my life; but I did not know I was so happy at the time."

"We think it is a very miserable story," said the rats. "Don't you know any story about bacon or tallow in the storeroom?"

"No," replied the tree.

"Many thanks to you, then," replied the rats, and they went their ways.

The little mice also kept away after this, and the tree sighed and said: "It was very pleasant when the merry little mice sat round me and listened while I talked. Now that is all past, too. However, I shall consider myself happy when some one comes to take me out of this place."

But would this ever happen? Yes; one morning people came to clear up the garret; the boxes were packed away, and the tree was pulled out of the corner and thrown roughly on the floor; then the servants dragged it out upon the staircase, where the daylight shone.

"Now life is beginning again," said the tree, rejoicing in the sunshine and fresh air. Then it was carried downstairs and taken into the courtyard so quickly that it forgot to think of itself and could only look about, there was so much to be seen.

The court was close to a garden, where everything looked blooming. Fresh and fragrant roses hung over the little palings. The linden trees were in blossom, while swallows flew here and there, crying, "Twit, twit, twit, my mate is coming"; but it was not the fir tree they meant.

"Now I shall live," cried the tree joyfully, spreading out its branches; but alas! they were all withered and yellow, and it lay in a corner among weeds and nettles. The star of gold paper still stuck in the top of the tree and glittered in the sunshine.

Two of the merry children who had danced round the tree at Christmas and had been so happy were playing in the same courtyard. The youngest saw the gilded star and ran and pulled it off the tree. "Look what is sticking to the ugly old fir tree," said the child, treading on the branches till they crackled under his boots.

And the tree saw all the fresh, bright flowers in the garden and then looked at itself and wished it had remained in the dark corner of the garret. It thought of its fresh youth in the forest, of the merry Christmas evening, and of the little mice who had listened to the story of Humpty Dumpty.

"Past! past!" said the poor tree. "Oh, had I but enjoyed myself while I could have done so! but now it is too late."

Then a lad came and chopped the tree into small pieces, till a large bundle lay in a heap on the ground. The pieces were placed in a fire, and they quickly blazed up brightly, while the tree sighed so deeply that each sigh was like a little pistol shot. Then the children who were at play came and seated themselves in front of the fire, and looked at it and cried, "Pop, pop." But at each "pop," which was a deep sigh, the tree was thinking of a summer day in the forest or of some winter night there when the stars shone brightly, and of Christmas evening, and of Humpty Dumpty—the only story it had ever heard or knew how to relate—till at last it was consumed.

The boys still played in the garden, and the youngest

wore on his breast the golden star with which the tree had been adorned during the happiest evening of its existence. Now all was past; the tree's life was past and the story also past—for all stories must come to an end at some time or other.

MARY'S SONG

George MacDonald

Babe Jesus lay in Mary's lap;
    The sun shone in his hair;
And this was how she saw, mayhap,
    The crown already there.

For she sang: "Sleep on, my little king,
    Bad Herod dares not come;
Before thee sleeping, holy thing,
    The wild winds would be dumb.

"I kiss thy hands, I kiss thy feet,
    My child, so long desired;

Thy hands will never be soiled, my sweet;
    Thy feet will never be tired.

"For thou art the king of men, my son;
    Thy crown I see it plain!
And men shall worship thee, every one,
    And cry, Glory! Amen!"

Babe Jesus opened his eyes so wide!
    At Mary looked her Lord.
Mother Mary stinted her song and sighed.
    Babe Jesus said never a word.

THE MAGI

W. B. Yeats

Now as at all times I can see in the mind's eye,

In their stiff, painted clothes, the pale unsatisfied ones

Appear and disappear in the blue depth of the sky

With all their ancient faces like rain-beaten
    stones,

And all their helms of silver hovering side by side,

And all their eyes still fixed, hoping to find once
    more,

Being by Calvary's turbulence unsatisfied,

The uncontrollable mystery on the bestial floor.

A Christmas Dream, and How It Came to Be True

Louisa May Alcott

"I'm so tired of Christmas I wish there never would be another one!" exclaimed a discontented-looking little girl, as she sat idly watching her mother arrange a pile of gifts two days before they were to be given.

"Why, Effie, what a dreadful thing to say! You are as bad as old Scrooge; and I'm afraid something will happen to you, as it did to him, if you don't care for dear Christmas," answered mamma, almost dropping the silver horn she was filling with delicious candies.

"Who was Scrooge? What happened to him?" asked Effie, with a glimmer of interest in her listless face, as she picked out the sourest lemon-drop she could find; for nothing sweet suited her just then.

"He was one of Dickens's best people, and you can read the charming story some day. He hated Christmas until a strange dream showed him how dear and beautiful it was, and made a better man of him."

"I shall read it; for I like dreams, and have a great many curious ones myself. But they don't keep me from being tired of Christmas," said Effie, poking discontentedly among the sweeties for something worth eating.

"Why are you tired of what should be the happiest time of all the year?" asked mamma, anxiously.

"Perhaps I shouldn't be if I had something new. But it is always the same, and there isn't any more surprise about it. I always find heaps of goodies in my stocking. Don't like some of them, and soon get tired of those I do like. We always have a great dinner, and I eat too much, and feel ill next day. Then there is a Christmas tree somewhere, with a doll on top, or a stupid old Santa Claus, and children dancing and screaming over bonbons and toys that break, and shiny things that are of no use. Really, mamma, I've had so many Christmases all alike that I don't think I can bear another one." And Effie laid herself flat on the sofa, as if the mere idea was too much for her.

Her mother laughed at her despair, but was sorry to see her little girl so discontented, when she had everything to make her happy, and had known but ten Christmas days.

"Suppose we don't give you any presents at all,—how would that suit you?" asked mamma, anxious to please her spoiled child.

"I should like one large and splendid one, and one dear little one, to remember some very nice person by," said Effie, who was a fanciful little body, full of odd whims and notions, which her friends loved to gratify, regardless of time, trouble, or money; for she was the last of three little girls, and very dear to all the family.

"Well, my darling, I will see what I can do to please you, and not say a word until all is ready. If I could only get a new idea to start with!" And mamma went on tying up her pretty bundles with a thoughtful face, while Effie strolled to the window to watch the rain that kept her in-doors and made her dismal.

"Seems to me poor children have better times than rich ones. I can't go out, and there is a girl about my age splashing along, without any maid to fuss about rubbers and cloaks and umbrellas and colds. I wish I was a beggar-girl."

"Would you like to be hungry, cold, and ragged, to beg all day, and sleep on an ash-heap at night?" asked mamma, wondering what would come next.

"Cinderella did, and had a nice time in the end. This girl out here has a basket of scraps on her arm, and a big old shawl all round her, and doesn't seem to care a bit, though the water runs out of the toes of her boots. She goes paddling along, laughing at the rain, and eating a cold potato as if it tasted nicer than the chicken and ice-cream I had for dinner. Yes, I do think poor children are happier than rich ones."

"So do I, sometimes. At the Orphan Asylum today I saw two dozen merry little souls who have no parents, no home, and no hope of Christmas beyond a stick of candy or a cake. I wish you had been there to see how happy they were, playing with the old toys some richer children had sent them."

"You may give them all mine; I'm so tired of them I never want to see them again," said Effie, turning from the window to the pretty baby-house full of everything a child's heart could desire.

"I will, and let you begin again with something you will not tire of, if I can only find it." And mamma knit her brows trying to discover some grand surprise for this child who didn't care for Christmas.

Nothing more was said then; and wandering off to the library, Effie found *A Christmas Carol*, and curling herself up in the sofa corner, read it all before tea. Some of it she did not understand; but she laughed and cried over many parts of the charming story, and felt better without knowing why.

All the evening she thought of poor Tiny Tim, Mrs. Cratchit with the pudding, and the stout old gentleman who danced so gayly that "his legs twinkled in the air." Presently bedtime arrived.

"Come, now, and toast your feet," said Effie's nurse, "while I do your pretty hair and tell stories." "I'll have a fairy tale to-night, a very interesting one," commanded Effie, as she put on her blue silk wrapper and little fur-lined slippers to sit before the fire and have her long curls brushed.

So Nursey told her best tales; and when at last the child lay down under her lace curtains, her head was full of a curious jumble of Christmas elves, poor children, snow-storms, sugarplums, and surprises. So it is no wonder that she dreamed all night; and this was the dream, which she never quite forgot.

She found herself sitting on a stone, in the middle of a great field, all alone. The snow was falling fast, a bitter wind whistled by, and night was coming on. She felt hungry, cold, and tired, and did not know where to go nor what to do.

"I wanted to be a beggar-girl, and now I am one; but I don't like it, and wish somebody would come and take care of me. I don't know who I am, and I think I must be lost," thought Effie, with the curious interest one takes in one's self in dreams. But the more she thought about it, the more bewildered she felt. Faster fell the snow, colder blew the wind, darker grew the night; and poor Effie made up her mind that she was quite forgotten and left to freeze alone. The tears were chilled on her cheeks, her feet felt like icicles, and her heart died within her, so hungry, frightened, and forlorn was she. Laying her head on her knees, she gave herself up for lost, and sat there with the great flakes fast turning her to a little white mound, when suddenly the sound of music reached her, and starting up, she looked and listened with all her eyes and ears.

Far away a dim light shone, and a voice was heard singing. She tried to run toward the welcome glimmer, but could not stir, and stood like a small statue of expectation while the light drew nearer, and the sweet words of the song grew clearer.

From our happy home
Through the world we roam
One week in all the year,

132

Making winter spring
With the joy we bring,
For Christmas-tide is here.
Now the eastern star
Shines from afar
To light the poorest home;
Hearts warmer grow,
Gifts freely flow,
For Christmas-tide has come.
Now gay trees rise
Before young eyes,
Abloom with tempting cheer;
Blithe voices sing,
And blithe bells ring,
For Christmas-tide is here.
Oh, happy chime,
Oh, blessed time,
That draws us all so near!
"Welcome, dear day,"
All creatures say,
For Christmas-tide is here.

A child's voice sang, a child's hand carried the little candle; and in the circle of soft light it shed, Effie saw a pretty child coming to her through the night and snow. A rosy, smiling creature, wrapped in white fur, with a wreath of green and scarlet holly on its shining hair, the magic candle in one hand, and the other outstretched as if to shower gifts and warmly press all other hands.

Effie forgot to speak as this bright vision came nearer, leaving no trace of footsteps in the snow, only lighting the way with its little candle, and filling the air with the music of its song.

"Dear child, you are lost, and I have come to find you," said the stranger, taking Effie's cold hands in his, with a smile like sunshine, while every holly berry glowed like a little fire.

"Do you know me?" asked Effie, feeling no fear, but a great gladness, at his coming.

"I know all children, and go to find them; for this is my holiday, and I gather them from all parts of the world to be merry with me once a year."

"Are you an angel?" asked Effie, looking for the wings.

"No; I am a Christmas spirit, and live with my mates in a pleasant place, getting ready for our holiday, when we are let out to roam about the world, helping make this a happy time for all who will let us in. Will you come and see how we work?" "I will go anywhere with you. Don't leave me again," cried Effie, gladly.

"First I will make you comfortable. That is what we love to do. You are cold, and you shall be warm, hungry, and I will feed you; sorrowful, and I will make you gay."

With a wave of his candle all three miracles were wrought,—for the snow-flakes turned to a white fur cloak and hood on Effie's head and shoulders, a bowl of hot soup came sailing to her lips, and vanished when she had eagerly drunk the last drop; and suddenly the dismal field changed to a new world so full of wonders that all her troubles were forgotten in a minute. Bells were ringing so merrily that it was hard to keep from dancing. Green garlands hung on the walls, and every tree was a Christmas tree full of toys, and blazing with candles that never went out.

In one place many little spirits sewed like mad on warm clothes, turning off work faster than any sewing-machine ever invented, and great piles were made ready to be sent to poor people. Other busy creatures packed money into purses, and wrote checks which they sent flying away on the wind,—a lovely kind of snow-storm to fall into a world below full of poverty. Older and graver spirits were looking over piles of little books, in which the records of the past year were kept, telling how different people had spent it, and what sort of gifts they deserved. Some got peace, some disappointment, some remorse and sorrow, some great joy and hope. The rich had generous thoughts sent them; the poor, gratitude and contentment. Children had more love and duty to parents; and parents renewed patience, wisdom, and satisfaction for and in their children. No one was forgotten.

"Please tell me what splendid place this is?" asked Effie, as soon as she could collect her wits after the first look at all these astonishing things.

"This is the Christmas world; and here we work all the year round, never tired of getting ready for the happy day. See, these are the saints just setting off; for some have far to go, and the children must not be disappointed."

As he spoke the spirit pointed to four gates, out of which four great sleighs were just driving, laden with toys, while a jolly old Santa Claus sat in the middle of each, drawing on his mittens and tucking up his wraps for a long cold drive. "Why, I thought there was only one Santa Claus, and even he was a humbug," cried Effie, astonished at the sight.

"Never give up your faith in the sweet old stones, even after you come to see that they are only the pleasant shadow of a lovely truth."

Just then the sleighs went off with a great jingling of bells and pattering of reindeer hoofs, while all the spirits gave a cheer that was heard in the lower world, where people said, "Hear the stars sing."

"I never will say there isn't any Santa Claus again. Now, show me more."

"You will like to see this place, I think, and may learn something here perhaps."

The spirit smiled as he led the way to a little door, through which Effie peeped into a world of dolls. Baby-houses were in full blast, with dolls of all sorts going on like live people. Waxen ladies sat in their parlors elegantly dressed; black dolls cooked in the kitchens; nurses walked out with the bits of dollies; and the streets were full of tin soldiers marching, wooden horses prancing, express wagons rumbling, and little men hurrying to and fro. Shops were there, and tiny people buying legs of mutton, pounds of tea, mites of clothes, and everything dolls use or wear or want.

But presently she saw that in some ways the dolls improved upon the manners and customs of human beings, and she watched eagerly to learn why they did these things. A fine Paris doll driving in her carriage took up a black worsted Dinah who was hobbling along with a basket of clean clothes, and carried her to her journey's end, as if it were the proper thing to do. Another interesting china lady took off her comfortable red cloak and put it round a poor wooden creature done up in a paper shift, and so badly painted that its face would have sent some babies into fits.

"Seems to me I once knew a rich girl who didn't give her things to poor girls. I wish I could remember who she was, and tell her to be as kind as that china doll," said Effie, much touched at the sweet way the pretty creature wrapped up the poor fright, and then ran off in her little gray gown to buy a shiny fowl stuck on a wooden platter for her invalid mother's dinner.

"We recall these things to people's minds by dreams. I think the girl you speak of won't forget this one." And the spirit smiled, as if he enjoyed some joke which she did not see.

A little bell rang as she looked, and away scampered the children into the red-and-green school-house with the roof that lifted up, so one could see how nicely they sat at their desks with mites of books, or drew on the inch-square blackboards with crumbs of chalk.

"They know their lessons very well, and are as still as mice. We make a great racket at our school, and get bad marks every day. I shall tell the girls they had better mind what they do, or their dolls will be better scholars than they are," said Effie, much impressed, as she peeped in and saw no rod in the hand of the little mistress, who looked up and shook her head at the intruder, as if begging her to go away before the order of the school was disturbed.

Effie retired at once, but could not resist one look in at the window of a fine mansion, where the family were at dinner, the children behaved so well at table, and never grumbled a bit when their mamma said they could not have any more fruit. "Now, show me something else," she said, as they came again to the low door that led out of Doll-land.

"You have seen how we prepare for Christmas; let me show you where we love best to send our good and happy gifts," answered the spirit, giving her his hand again.

"I know. I've seen ever so many," began Effie, thinking of her own Christmases.

"No, you have never seen what I will show you. Come away, and remember what you see to-night."

Like a flash that bright world vanished, and Effie found herself in a part of the city she had never seen before. It was far away from the gayer places, where every store was brilliant with lights and full of pretty things, and every house wore a festival air, while people hurried to and fro with merry greetings. It was down among the dingy streets where the poor lived, and where there was no making ready for Christmas.

Hungry women looked in at the shabby shops, longing to buy meat and bread, but empty pockets forbade. Tipsy men drank up their wages in the bar-rooms; and in many cold dark chambers little children huddled under the thin blankets, trying to forget their misery in sleep.

No nice dinners filled the air with savory smells, no gay trees dropped toys and bonbons into eager hands, no little stockings hung in rows beside the chimney-piece ready to be filled, no happy sounds of music, gay voices, and dancing feet were heard; and there were no signs of Christmas anywhere.

"Don't they have any in this place?" asked Effie, shivering, as she held fast the spirit's hand, following where he led her.

"We come to bring it. Let me show you our best workers." And the spirit pointed to some sweet-faced men and women who came stealing into the poor houses, working such beautiful miracles that Effie could only stand and watch.

Some slipped money into the empty pockets, and sent the happy mothers to buy all the comforts they needed; others led the drunken men out of temptation, and took them home to find safer pleasures there. Fires were kindled on cold hearths, tables spread as if by magic, and warm clothes wrapped round shivering limbs. Flowers suddenly bloomed in the chambers of the sick; old people found themselves remembered; sad hearts were consoled by a tender word, and wicked ones softened by the story of Him who forgave all sin.

But the sweetest work was for the children; and Effie held her breath to watch these human fairies hang up and fill the little stockings without which a child's Christmas is not perfect, putting in things that once she would have thought very humble presents, but which now seemed beautiful and precious because these poor babies had nothing.

"That is so beautiful! I wish I could make merry Christmases as these good people do, and be loved and thanked as they are," said Effie, softly, as she watched the busy men and women do their work and steal away without thinking of any reward but their own satisfaction.

"You can if you will. I have shown you the way. Try it, and see how happy your own holiday will be hereafter."

As he spoke, the spirit seemed to put his arms about her, and vanished with a kiss.

"Oh, stay and show me more!" cried Effie, trying to hold him fast.

"Darling, wake up, and tell me why you are smiling in your sleep," said a voice in her ear; and opening her eyes, there was mamma bending over her, and morning sunshine streaming into the room.

"Are they all gone? Did you hear the bells? Wasn't it splendid?" she asked, rubbing her eyes, and looking about her for the pretty child who was so real and sweet.

"You have been dreaming at a great rate,—talking in your sleep, laughing, and clapping your hands as if you were cheering some one. Tell me what was so splendid," said mamma, smoothing the tumbled hair and lifting up the sleepy head. Then, while she was being dressed, Effie told her dream, and Nursey thought it very wonderful; but mamma smiled to see how curiously things the child had thought, read, heard, and seen through the day were mixed up in her sleep.

"The spirit said I could work lovely miracles if I tried; but I don't know how to begin, for I have no magic candle to make feasts appear, and light up groves of Christmas trees, as he did," said Effie, sorrowfully.

"Yes, you have. We will do it! we will do it!" And clapping her hands, mamma suddenly began to dance all over the room as if she had lost her wits.

"How? how? You must tell me, mamma," cried Effie, dancing after her, and ready to believe anything possible when she remembered the adventures of the past night.

"I've got it! I've got it!—the new idea. A splendid one, if I can only carry it out!" And mamma waltzed the little girl round till her curls flew wildly in the air, while Nursey laughed as if she would die.

"Tell me! tell me!" shrieked Effie. "No, no; it is a surprise,—a grand surprise for Christmas day!" sung mamma, evidently charmed with her happy thought. "Now, come to breakfast; for we must work like bees if we want to play spirits tomorrow. You and Nursey will go out shopping, and get heaps of things, while I arrange matters behind the scenes."

They were running downstairs as mamma spoke, and Effie called out breathlessly,—

"It won't be a surprise; for I know you are going to ask some poor children here, and have a tree or something. It won't be like my dream; for they had ever so many trees, and more children than we can find anywhere."

"There will be no tree, no party, no dinner, in this house at all, and no presents for you. Won't that be a surprise?" And mamma laughed at Effie's bewildered face.

"Do it. I shall like it, I think; and I won't ask any questions, so it will all burst upon me when the time comes," she said; and she ate her breakfast thoughtfully, for this really would be a new sort of Christmas.

All that morning Effie trotted after Nursey in and out of shops, buying dozens of barking dogs, woolly lambs, and squeaking birds; tiny tea-sets, gay picture-books, mittens and hoods, dolls and candy. Parcel after parcel was sent home; but when Effie returned she saw no trace of them, though she peeped everywhere. Nursey chuckled, but wouldn't give a hint, and went out again in the afternoon with a long list of more things to buy; while Effie wandered forlornly about the house, missing the usual merry stir that went before the Christmas dinner and the evening fun.

As for mamma, she was quite invisible all day, and came in at night so tired that she could only lie on the sofa to rest, smiling as if some very pleasant thought made her happy in spite of weariness.

"Is the surprise going on all right?" asked Effie, anxiously; for it seemed an immense time to wait till another evening came.

"Beautifully! better than I expected; for several of my good friends are helping, or I couldn't have done it as I wish. I know you will like it, dear, and long remember this new way of making Christmas merry."

Mamma gave her a very tender kiss, and Effie went to bed.

The next day was a very strange one; for when she woke there was no stocking to examine, no pile of gifts under her napkin, no one said "Merry Christmas!" to her, and the dinner was just as usual to her. Mamma vanished again, and

Nursey kept wiping her eyes and saying: "The dear things! It's the prettiest idea I ever heard of. No one but your blessed ma could have done it." "Do stop, Nursey, or I shall go crazy because I don't know the secret!" cried Effie, more than once; and she kept her eye on the clock, for at seven in the evening the surprise was to come off.

The longed-for hour arrived at last, and the child was too excited to ask questions when Nurse put on her cloak and hood, led her to the carriage, and they drove away, leaving their house the one dark and silent one in the row. "I feel like the girls in the fairy tales who are led off to strange places and see fine things," said Effie, in a whisper, as they jingled through the gay streets.

"Ah, my deary, it is like a fairy tale, I do assure you, and you will see finer things than most children will tonight. Steady, now, and do just as I tell you, and don't say one word whatever you see," answered Nursey, quite quivering with excitement as she patted a large box in her lap, and nodded and laughed with twinkling eyes.

They drove into a dark yard, and Effie was led through a back door to a little room, where Nurse coolly proceeded to take off not only her cloak and hood, but her dress and shoes also. Effie stared and bit her lips, but kept still until out of the box came a little white fur coat and boots, a wreath of holly leaves and berries, and a candle with a frill of gold paper round it. A long "Oh!" escaped her then; and when she was dressed and saw herself in the glass, she started back, exclaiming, "Why, Nursey, I look like the spirit in my dream!"

"So you do; and that's the part you are to play, my pretty! Now whist, while I blind your eyes and put you in your place."

"Shall I be afraid?" whispered Effie, full of wonder; for as they went out she heard the sound of many voices, the tramp of many feet, and, in spite of the bandage, was sure a great light shone upon her when she stopped.

"You needn't be; I shall stand close by, and your ma will be there."

After the handkerchief was tied about her eyes, Nurse led Effie up some steps, and placed her on a high platform, where something like leaves touched her head, and the soft snap of lamps seemed to fill the air. Music began as soon as Nurse clapped her hands, the voices outside sounded nearer, and the tramp was evidently coming up the stairs.

"Now, my precious, look and see how you and your dear ma have made a merry Christmas for them that needed it!"

Off went the bandage; and for a minute Effie really did think she was asleep again, for she actually stood in "a grove of Christmas trees," all gay and shining as in her vision. Twelve on a side, in two rows down the room, stood the little pines, each on its low table; and behind Effie a taller one rose to the roof, hung with wreaths of popcorn, apples, oranges, horns of candy, and cakes of all sorts, from sugary hearts to gingerbread Jumbos. On the smaller trees she saw many of her own discarded toys and those Nursey bought, as well as heaps that seemed to have rained down straight from that delightful Christmas country where she felt as if she was again.

"How splendid! Who is it for? What is that noise? Where is mamma?" cried Effie, pale with pleasure and surprise, as she stood looking down the brilliant little street from her high place.

Before Nurse could answer, the doors at the lower end flew open, and in marched twenty-four little blue-gowned orphan girls, singing sweetly, until amazement changed the song to cries of joy and wonder as the shining spectacle appeared. While they stood staring with round eyes at the wilderness of pretty things about them, mamma stepped up beside Effie, and holding her hand fast to give her courage, told the story of the dream in a few simple words, ending in this way:—

"So my little girl wanted to be a Christmas spirit too, and make this a happy day for those who had not as many pleasures and comforts as she has. She likes surprises, and we planned this for you all. She shall play the good fairy, and give each of you something from this tree, after which every one will find her own name on a small tree, and can go to enjoy it in her own way. March by, my dears, and let us fill your hands."

Nobody told them to do it, but all the hands were clapped heartily before a single child stirred; then one by one they came to look up wonderingly at the pretty giver of the feast as she leaned down to offer them great yellow oranges, red apples, bunches of grapes, bonbons, and cakes, till all were gone, and a double row of smiling faces turned toward her as the children filed back to their places in the orderly way they had been taught.

Then each was led to her own tree by the good ladies who had helped mamma with all their hearts; and the happy hubbub that arose would have satisfied even Santa Claus himself,—shrieks of joy, dances of delight, laughter and tears (for some tender little things could not bear so much pleasure at once, and sobbed with mouths full of candy and hands full of toys). How they ran to show one another the new treasures! how they peeped and tasted, pulled and pinched, until the air was full of queer noises, the floor covered with papers, and the little trees left bare of all but candles!

"I don't think heaven can be any gooder than this," sighed one small girl, as she looked about her in a blissful maze, holding her full apron with one hand, while she luxuriously carried sugar-plums to her mouth with the other.

"Is that a truly angel up there?" asked another, fascinated by the little white figure with the wreath on its shining hair, who in some mysterious way had been the cause of all this merry-making.

"I wish I dared to go and kiss her for this splendid party," said a lame child, leaning on her crutch, as she stood near the steps, wondering how it seemed to sit in a mother's lap, as Effie was doing, while she watched the happy scene before her. Effie heard her, and remembering Tiny Tim, ran down and put her arms about the pale child, kissing the wistful face, as she said sweetly, "You may; but mamma deserves the thanks. She did it all; I only dreamed about it."

Lame Katy felt as if "a truly angel" was embracing her, and could only stammer out her thanks, while the other children ran to see the pretty spirit, and touch her soft dress, until she stood in a crowd of blue gowns laughing as they held up their gifts for her to see and admire.

Mamma leaned down and whispered one word to the older girls; and suddenly they all took hands to dance round Effie, singing as they skipped.

It was a pretty sight, and the ladies found it hard to break up the happy revel; but it was late for small people, and too much fun is a mistake. So the girls fell into line, and marched before Effie and mamma again, to say goodnight with such grateful little faces that the eyes of those who looked grew dim with tears. Mamma kissed every one; and many a hungry childish heart felt as if the touch of those tender lips was their best gift. Effie shook so many small hands that her own tingled; and when Katy came she pressed a small doll into Effie's hand, whispering, "You didn't have a single present, and we had lots. Do keep that; it's the prettiest thing I got."

"I will," answered Effie, and held it fast until the last smiling face was gone, the surprise all over, and she safe in her own bed, too tired and happy for anything but sleep.

"Mamma, it was a beautiful surprise, and I thank you so much! I don't see how you did it; but I like it best of all the Christmases I ever had, and mean to make one every year. I had my splendid big present, and here is the dear little one to keep for love of poor Katy; so even that part of my wish came true."

And Effie fell asleep with a happy smile on her lips, her one humble gift still in her hand, and a new love for Christmas in her heart that never changed through a long life spent in doing good.

CHRISTMAS EVE

Christina Rossetti

Christmas hath a darkness
      Brighter than the blazing noon,
Christmas hath a chillness
      Warmer than the heat of June,
Christmas hath a beauty
      Lovelier than the world can show:
For Christmas bringeth Jesus,
      Brought for us so low.

Earth, strike up your music,
      Birds that sing and bells that ring;
Heaven hath answering music

For all Angels soon to sing:
Earth, put on your whitest
Bridal robe of spotless snow
For Christmas bringeth Jesus,
Brought for us so low.

THE CHRISTMAS SILENCE

Margaret Deland

Hushed are the pigeons cooing low,
On dusty rafters of the loft;
And mild-eyed oxen, breathing soft,
Sleep on the fragrant hay below.

Dim shadows in the corner hide;
The glimmering lantern's rays are shed
Where one young lamb just lifts his head,
Then huddles 'gainst his mother's side.

Strange silence tingles in the air;
Through the half-open door a bar

Of light from one low hanging star
Touches a baby's radiant hair—

No sound—the mother, kneeling, lays
Her cheek against the little face.
Oh human love! Oh heavenly grace!
'Tis yet in silence that she prays!

Ages of silence end to-night;
Then to the long-expectant earth
Glad angels come to greet His birth
In burst of music, love, and light!

THE JOSEPHS' CHRISTMAS

L. M. Montgomery

The month before Christmas was always the most exciting and mysterious time in the Joseph household. Such scheming and planning, such putting of curly heads together in corners, such counting of small hoards, such hiding and smuggling of things out of sight, as went on among the little Josephs!

There were a good many of them, and very few of the pennies; hence the reason for so much contriving and consulting. From fourteen-year-old Mollie down to four-year-old Lennie there were eight small Josephs in all in the little log house on the prairie; so that when each little Joseph wanted to give a Christmas box to each of the other little

Josephs, and something to Father and Mother Joseph be-sides, it is no wonder that they had to cudgel their small brains for ways and means thereof.

Father and Mother were always discreetly blind and si-lent through December. No questions were asked no matter what queer things were done. Many secret trips to the little store at the railway station two miles away were ignored, and no little Joseph was called to account because he or she looked terribly guilty when somebody suddenly came into the room. The air was simply charged with secrets.

Sister Mollie was the grand repository of these; all the little Josephs came to her for advice and assistance. It was Mollie who for troubled small brothers and sisters did such sums in division as this: How can I get a ten-cent present for Emmy and a fifteen-cent one for Jimmy out of eighteen cents? Or, how can seven sticks of candy be divided among eight people so that each shall have one? It was Mollie who advised regarding the purchase of ribbon and crepe pa-per. It was Mollie who put the finishing touches to most of the little gifts. In short, all through December Mollie was weighed down under an avalanche of responsibility. It speaks volumes for her sagacity and skill that she never got things mixed up or made any such terrible mistake as let-ting one little Joseph find out what another was going to give him. "Dead" secrecy was the keystone of all plans and confidences.

During this particular December the planning and contriving had been more difficult and the results less satisfactory than usual. The Josephs were poor at any time, but this winter they were poorer than ever. The crops had failed in the summer, and as a consequence the family were, as Jimmy said, "on short commons." But they made the brave best of their small resources, and on Christmas Eve every little Joseph went to bed with a clear conscience, for was there not on the corner table in the kitchen a small mountain of tiny—sometimes very tiny—gifts labelled with the names of recipients and givers, and worth their weight in gold if love and good wishes count for anything?

It was beginning to snow when the small small Josephs went to bed, and when the big small Josephs climbed the stairs it was snowing thickly. Mr. and Mrs. Joseph sat before the fire and listened to the wind howling about the house.

"I'm glad I'm not driving over the prairie tonight," said Mr. Joseph. "It's quite a storm. I hope it will be fine tomorrow, for the children's sake. They've set their hearts on having a sleigh ride, and it will be too bad if they can't have it when it's about all the Christmas they'll have this year. Mary, this is the first Christmas since we came west that we couldn't afford some little extras for them, even if 'twas only a box of nuts and candy."

Mrs. Joseph sighed over Jimmy's worn jacket which she was mending. Then she smiled.

"Never mind, John. Things will be better next Christmas, we'll hope. The children will not mind, bless their hearts. Look at all the little knick-knacks they've made for each other. Last week when I was over at Taunton, Mr. Fisher had his store all 'gayified up,' as Jim says, with Christmas presents. I did feel that I'd ask nothing better than to go in and buy all the lovely things I wanted, just for once, and give them to the children tomorrow morning. They've never had anything really nice for Christmas. But there! We've all got each other and good health and spirits, and a Christmas wouldn't be much without those if we had all the presents in the world."

Mr. Joseph nodded.

"That's so. I don't want to grumble; but I tell you I did want to get Maggie a 'real live doll,' as she calls it. She never has had anything but homemade dolls, and that small heart of hers is set on a real one. There was one at Fisher's store today—a big beauty with real hair, and eyes that opened and shut. Just fancy Maggie's face if she saw such a Christmas box as that tomorrow morning."

"Don't let's fancy it," laughed Mrs. Joseph, "it is only aggravating. Talking of candy reminds me that I made a big plateful of taffy for the children today. It's all the 'Christmassy' I could give them. I'll get it out and put it on the table along with the children's presents. That can't be someone at the door!"

"It is, though," said Mr. Joseph as he strode to the door and flung it open.

Two snowed-up figures were standing on the porch. As they stepped in, the Josephs recognized one of them as Mr. Ralston, a wealthy merchant in a small town fifteen miles away.

"Late hour for callers, isn't it?" said Mr. Ralston. "The fact is, our horse has about given out, and the storm is so bad that we can't proceed. This is my wife, and we are on our way to spend Christmas with my brother's family at Lindsay. Can you take us in for the night, Mr. Joseph?"

"Certainly, and welcome!" exclaimed Mr. Joseph heartily, "if you don't mind a shakedown by the kitchen fire for the night. My, Mrs. Ralston," as his wife helped her off with her things, "but you are snowed up! I'll see to putting your horse away, Mr. Ralston. This way, if you please."

When the two men came stamping into the house again Mrs. Ralston and Mrs. Joseph were sitting at the fire, the former with a steaming hot cup of tea in her hand. Mr.

Ralston put the big basket he was carrying down on a bench in the corner.

"Thought I'd better bring our Christmas flummery in," he said. "You see, Mrs. Joseph, my brother has a big family, so we are taking them a lot of Santa Claus stuff. Mrs. Ralston packed this basket, and goodness knows what she put in it, but she half cleaned out my store. The eyes of the Lindsay youngsters will dance tomorrow—that is, if we ever get there."

Mrs. Joseph gave a little sigh in spite of herself, and looked wistfully at the heap of gifts on the corner table. How meagre and small they did look, to be sure, beside that bulgy basket with its cover suggestively tied down.

Mrs. Ralston looked too.

"Santa Claus seems to have visited you already," she said with a smile.

The Josephs laughed.

"Our Santa Claus is somewhat out of pocket this year," said Mr. Joseph frankly. "Those are the little things the small folks here have made for each other. They've been a month at it, and I'm always kind of relieved when Christmas is over and there are no more mysterious doings. We're in such cramped quarters here that you can't move without stepping on somebody's secret."

A shakedown was spread in the kitchen for the unexpected guests, and presently the Ralstons found themselves alone. Mrs. Ralston went over to the Christmas table and looked at the little gifts half tenderly and half pityingly.

"They're not much like the contents of our basket, are they?" she said, as she touched the calendar Jimmie had made for Mollie out of cardboard and autumn leaves and grasses.

"Just what I was thinking," returned her husband, "and I was thinking of something else, too. I've a notion that I'd like to see some of the things in our basket right here on this table."

"I'd like to see them all," said Mrs. Ralston promptly. "Let's just leave them here, Edward. Roger's family will have plenty of presents without them, and for that matter we can send them ours when we go back home."

"Just as you say," agreed Mr. Ralston. "I like the idea of giving the small folk of this household a rousing good Christmas for once. They're poor I know, and I dare say pretty well pinched this year like most of the farmers hereabout after the crop failure."

Mrs. Ralston untied the cover of the big basket. Then the two of them, moving as stealthily as if engaged in a burglary, transferred the contents to the table. Mr. Ralston got out a small pencil and a note book, and by dint of comparing the names attached to the gifts on the table they managed to divide theirs up pretty evenly among the little Josephs.

When all was done Mrs. Ralston said, "Now, I'm going to spread that tablecloth carelessly over the table. We will be going before daylight, probably, and in the hurry of getting off I hope that Mr. and Mrs. Joseph will not notice the difference till we're gone."

It fell out as Mrs. Ralston had planned. The dawn broke fine and clear over a vast white world. Mr. and Mrs. Joseph were early astir; breakfast for the storm-stayed travellers was cooked and eaten by lamplight; then the horse and sleigh were brought to the door and Mr. Ralston carried out his empty basket.

"I expect the trail will be heavy," he said, "but I guess we'd get to Lindsay in time for dinner, anyway. Much obliged for your kindness, Mr. Joseph. When you and Mrs. Joseph come to town we shall hope to have a chance to return it. Good-bye and a merry Christmas to you all."

When Mrs. Joseph went back to the kitchen her eyes fell on the heaped-up table in the corner.

"Why-y!" she said, and snatched off the cover.

One look she gave, and then this funny little mother

began to cry; but they were happy tears. Mr. Joseph came too, and looked and whistled.

There really seemed to be everything on that table that the hearts of children could desire—three pairs of skates, a fur cap and collar, a dainty workbasket, half a dozen gleaming new books, a writing desk, a roll of stuff that looked like a new dress, a pair of fur-topped kid gloves just Mollie's size, and a china cup and saucer. All these were to be seen at the first glance; and in one corner of the table was a big box filled with candies and nuts and raisins, and in the other a doll with curling golden hair and brown eyes, dressed in "real" clothes and with all her wardrobe in a trunk beside her. Pinned to her dress was a leaf from Mr. Ralston's notebook with Maggie's name written on it.

"Well, this is Christmas with a vengeance," said Mr. Joseph.

"The children will go wild with delight," said his wife happily.

They pretty nearly did when they all came scrambling down the stairs a little later. Such a Christmas had never been known in the Joseph household before. Maggie clasped her doll with shining eyes, Mollie looked at the workbasket that her housewifely little heart had always longed for, studious Jimmy beamed over the books, and Ted and Hal whooped with delight over the skates. And as for the big box of good things, why, everybody appreciated that. That Christmas was one to date from in that family.

I'm glad to be able to say, too, that even in the heyday of their delight and surprise over their wonderful presents, the little Josephs did not forget to appreciate the gifts they had prepared for each other. Mollie thought her calendar just too pretty for anything, and Jimmy was sure the new red mittens which Maggie had knitted for him with her own chubby wee fingers, were the very nicest, gayest mittens a boy had ever worn.

Mrs. Joseph's taffy was eaten too. Not a scrap of it was left. As Ted said loyally, "It was just as good as the candy in the box and had more 'chew' to it besides."

CHRISTMAS CAROL

Paul Laurence Dunbar

Ring out, ye bells!
    All Nature swells
With gladness at the wondrous story,—
    The world was lorn,
    But Christ is born
To change our sadness into glory.

    Sing, earthlings, sing!
    To-night a King
Hath come from heaven's high throne to
    bless us.
    The outstretched hand

O'er all the land
Is raised in pity to caress us.

Come at his call;
Be joyful all;
Away with mourning and with sadness!
The heavenly choir
With holy fire
Their voices raise in songs of gladness.

The darkness breaks
And Dawn awakes,
Her cheeks suffused with youthful blushes.
The rocks and stones
In holy tones
Are singing sweeter than the thrushes.

Then why should we
In silence be,
When Nature lends her voice to praises;
When heaven and earth
Proclaim the truth
Of Him for whom that lone star blazes?

No, be not still,

But with a will

Strike all your harps and set them ringing;

On hill and heath

Let every breath

Throw all its power into singing!

O Little Town
of Bethlehem

Phillips Brooks

O little town of Bethlehem,

how still we see thee lie!

Above thy deep and dreamless sleep

the silent stars go by;

yet in thy dark streets shineth

the everlasting light.

The hopes and fears of all the years

are met in thee tonight.

For Christ is born of Mary,

and, gathered all above

while mortals sleep, the angels keep

their watch of wond'ring love.

O morning stars, together

proclaim the holy birth,

and praises sing to God the King

and peace to all the earth.

How silently, how silently,

the wondrous gift is giv'n!

So God imparts to human hearts

the blessings of his heav'n.

No ear may hear his coming,

but in this world of sin,

where meek souls will receive him, still

the dear Christ enters in.

O holy Child of Bethlehem,

descend to us, we pray,

cast out our sin and enter in,

be born in us today.

We hear the Christmas angels

the great glad tidings tell;

O come to us, abide with us,

our Lord Immanuel!

LITTLE GRETCHEN
AND THE WOODEN SHOE

Elizabeth Harrison

Once upon a time, a long time ago, far away across the great ocean, in a country called Germany, there could be seen a small log hut on the edge of a great forest, whose fir trees extended for miles and miles to the north. This little house, made of heavy hewn logs, had but one room in it. A rough pine door gave entrance to this room, and a small square window admitted the light. At the back of the house was built an old-fashioned stone chimney, out of which in winter curled a thin, blue smoke, showing that there was not very much fire within.

Small as the house was, it was large enough for two people who lived in it. I want to tell you a story today about these two people. One was an old gray-haired woman, so old that the little children of the village, nearly half a mile away, often wondered whether she had come into the world with the huge mountains and the giant fir trees, which stood like giants back of her small hut. Her face was wrinkled all over with deep lines, which, if the children could only have read aright, would have told them of many years of cheerful, happy, self-sacrifice; of loving, anxious, watching beside sick-beds; of quiet endurance of pain, of many a day of hunger and cold, and of a thousand deeds of unselfish love for other people; but, of course, they could not read this strange handwriting. They only knew that she was old and wrinkled, and that she stooped as she walked. None of them seemed to fear her, for her smile was always cheerful, and she had a kindly word for each of them if they chanced to meet her on her way to and from the village. With this old, old woman lived a very little girl. So bright and happy was she that the travellers who passed by the lonesome little house on the edge of the forest often thought of a sunbeam as they saw her. These two people were known in the village as Granny Goodyear and Little Gretchen.

The winter had come and the frost had snapped off many of the smaller branches of the pine trees in the forest. Gretchen and her granny were up by daybreak each morning. After their simple breakfast of oatmeal, Gretchen would run to the little closet and fetch Granny's old woolen shawl, which seemed almost as old as Granny herself. Gretchen always claimed the right to put the shawl over Granny's head, even though she had to climb onto the wooden bench to do it. After carefully pinning it under Granny's chin, she gave her a good-bye kiss, and Granny started out for her morning's work in the forest. This work was nothing more nor less than the gathering up of the twigs and branches which the autumn winds and winter frosts had thrown upon the ground. These were carefully gathered into a large bundle which Granny tied together with a strong linen band. She then managed to lift the bundle to her shoulder and trudged off to the village with it. Here she sold the fagots for kindling wood to the people of the village. Sometimes she would get only a few pence each day, and sometimes a dozen or more, but on this money little Gretchen and she managed to live; they had their home, and the forest kindly furnished the wood for the fire which kept them warm in winter.

In the summer time Granny had a little garden at the back of the house, where she raised, with little Gretchen's help, a few potatoes and turnips and onions. These she carefully stored away for winter use. To this meagre supply, the pennies, gained by selling the twigs from the forest, added the oatmeal for Gretchen and a little black coffee for Granny. Meat was a thing they never thought of having. It cost too much money. Still, Granny and Gretchen were very happy, because they loved each other dearly. Sometimes Gretchen would be left alone all day long in the hut, because Granny would have some work to do in the village after selling her bundle of sticks and twigs. It was during these long days that little Gretchen had taught herself to sing the song which the wind sang to the pine branches. In the summer time she learned the chirp and twitter of the birds, until her voice might almost be mistaken for a bird's voice, she learned to dance as the swaying shadows did, and even to talk to the stars which shone through the little square window when Granny came home late or too tired to talk.

Sometimes, when the weather was fine, or her Granny had an extra bundle of knitted stockings to take to the village, she would let little Gretchen go along with her. It chanced that one of these trips to the town came just the week before Christmas, and Gretchen's eyes were delighted by the sight of the lovely Christmas trees which stood in the window of the village store. It seemed to her that she would never tire of looking at the knit dolls, the woolly lambs, the little wooden shops with their queer, painted men and women in them, and all the other fine things. She had never owned a plaything in her whole life; therefore, toys which you and I would not think much of seemed to her very beautiful.

That night, after their supper of baked potatoes was over, and little Gretchen had cleared away the dishes and swept up the hearth, because Granny dear was so tired, she brought her own little wooden stool and placed it very near Granny's feet and sat down upon it, folding her hands on her lap. Granny knew that this meant that she wanted to be told about something, so she smilingly laid away the large Bible which she had been reading, and took up her knitting, which was as much as to say: "Well, Gretchen, dear, Granny is ready to listen."

"Granny," said Gretchen slowly, "it's almost Christmas time, isn't it?"

"Yes, dearie," said Granny, "only five days more now," and then she sighed, but little Gretchen was so happy that she did not notice Granny's sigh.

"What do you think, Granny, I'll get this Christmas?" said she, looking up eagerly into Granny's face.

"Ah, child, child," said Granny, shaking her head, "you'll have no Christmas this year. We are too poor for that."

"Oh, but Granny," interrupted little Gretchen, "think

of all the beautiful toys we saw in the village today. Surely Santa Claus has sent enough for every little child."

"Ah, dearie, those toys are for people who can pay for them, and we have no money to spend for Christmas toys."

"Well, Granny," said Gretchen, "perhaps some of the little children who live in the great house on the hill at the other end of the village, will be willing to share some of their toys with me. They will be glad to give some to a little girl who has none."

"Dear child, dear child," said Granny, leaning forward and stroking the soft, shiny hair of the little girl, "your heart is full of love. You would be glad to bring a Christmas to every child; but their heads are so full of what they are going to get that they forget all about anybody else but themselves." Then she sighed and shook her head.

"Well, Granny," said Gretchen, her bright, happy tone of voice growing a little less joyous, "perhaps the dear Santa Claus will show some of the village children how to make presents that do not cost money, and some of them may surprise me Christmas morning with a present. And, Granny, dear," added she, springing up from her low stool, "can't I gather some of the pine branches and take them to the old sick man who lives in the house by the mill, so that he can have the sweet smell of our forest in his room all Christmas day?"

"Yes, dearie," said Granny, "you may do what you can to make the Christmas bright and happy, but you must not expect any present yourself."

"Oh, but, Granny," said little Gretchen, her face brightening, "you forgot all about the shining Christmas angels, who came down to earth and sang their wonderful song the night the beautiful Christ-Child was born! They are so loving and good that they will not forget any little child. I shall ask my dear stars tonight to tell them of us. You know," she added, with a look of relief, "the stars are so very high that they must know the angels quite well as they come and go with their messages from the loving God."

Granny sighed as she half whispered. "Poor child, poor child!" but Gretchen threw her arm around Granny's neck and gave her a hearty kiss, saying as she did so: "Oh, Granny, Granny, you don't talk to the stars often enough, else you would not be sad at Christmas time." Then she danced all around the room, whirling her little skirts about her to show Granny how the wind had made the snow dance that day. She looked so droll and funny that Granny forgot her cares and worries and laughed with little Gretchen over her new snow dance. The days passed on and the morning before Christmas Eve came. Gretchen having tidied up the little room—for Granny had taught her to be a careful little housewife—was off to the forest, singing a birdlike song, almost as happy and free as the birds themselves. She was very busy that day preparing a surprise for Granny. First, however, she gathered the most beautiful of the fir branches within her reach to take the next morning to the old sick man who lived by the mill.

The day was all too short for the happy little girl. When Granny came trudging wearily home that night, she found the frame of the doorway covered with green pine branches.

"It is to welcome you, Granny! It is to welcome you!" cried Gretchen. "Our dear old home wanted to give you a Christmas welcome. Don't you see, the branches of the evergreen make it look as if it were smiling all over, and it is trying to say, 'A happy Christmas to you, Granny.'"

Granny laughed and kissed the little girl, as they opened the door and went in together. Here was a new surprise for Granny. The four posts of the wooden bed, which stood in one corner of the room, had been trimmed by the busy little fingers, with smaller and more flexible branches of the pine trees. A small bouquet of red mountain ash berries stood at each side of the fireplace, and these, together with the trimmed posts of the bed, gave the plain old room quite a festive look. Gretchen laughed and clapped her hands and danced about until the house seemed full of music to poor, tired Granny, whose heart had been sad as she turned toward their home that night, thinking of the disappointment that must come to loving little Gretchen the next morning.

After supper was over little Gretchen drew her stool up to Granny's side, and laying her soft, little hands on Granny's knee asked to be told once again the story of the coming of the Christ-Child; how the night that he was born the beautiful angels had sung their wonderful song, and how the whole sky had become bright with a strange and glorious light, never seen by the people of earth before. Gretchen had heard the story many, many times before, but she never grew tired of it, and now that Christmas Eve had come again, the happy little child wanted to hear it once more.

When Granny had finished telling it the two sat quiet and silent for a little while thinking it over; then Granny rose and said that it was time for her to go to bed. She slowly took off her heavy wooden shoes, such as are worn in that country, and placed them beside the hearth. Gretchen looked thoughtfully at them for a minute or two, and then she said, "Granny, don't you think that somebody in all this wide world will think of us tonight?"

"Nay, Gretchen, I do not think any one will."

"Well, then, Granny," said Gretchen, "the Christmas angels will, I know; so I am going to take one of your wooden shoes and put it on the windowsill outside, so that they may see it as they pass by. I am sure the stars will tell the Christmas angels where the shoe is."

"Ah, you foolish, foolish child," said Granny, "you are only getting ready for a disappointment. Tomorrow morning there will be nothing whatever in the shoe. I can tell you that now."

But little Gretchen would not listen. She only shook her head and cried out: "Ah, Granny, you do not talk enough to the stars." With this she seized the shoe, and opening the door, hurried out to place it on the window sill. It was very dark without and something soft and cold seemed to gently kiss her hair and face. Gretchen knew by this that it was snowing, and she looked up to the sky, anxious to see if the stars were in sight, but a strong wind was tumbling the dark, heavy snow-clouds about and had shut away all else.

"Never mind," said Gretchen softly to herself, "the stars are up there, even if I can't see them, and the Christmas angels do not mind snow storms."

Just then a rough wind went sweeping by the little girl, whispering something to her which she could not understand, and then it made a sudden rush up to the snow clouds and parted them, so that the deep mysterious sky appeared beyond, and shining down out of the midst of it was Gretchen's favorite star.

"Ah, little star, little star!" said the child, laughing aloud. "I knew you were there, though I could not see you. Will you whisper to the Christmas angels as they come by that little Gretchen wants so very much to have a Christmas gift tomorrow morning, if they have one to spare, and that she has put one of Granny's shoes upon the windowsill for it?"

A moment more and the little girl, standing on tiptoe had reached the windowsill and placed the shoe upon it, and was back again in the house beside Granny and the warm fire.

The two went quietly to bed, and that night as little Gretchen knelt to pray to the Heavenly Father, she thanked him for having sent the Christ-Child into the world to teach all mankind to be loving and unselfish, and in a few minutes she was sleeping, dreaming of the Christmas angels.

The next morning, very early, even before the sun was up, little Gretchen was awakened by the sound of sweet music coming from the village. She listened for a moment and then she knew that the choir boys were singing the Christmas carols in the open air of the village street.

She sprang up out of bed and began to dress herself as quickly as possible, singing as she dressed. While Granny was slowly putting on her clothes, little Gretchen having finished dressing herself, unfastened the door and hurried out to see what the Christmas angels had left in the old wooden shoe.

The white snow covered everything—trees, stumps, roads, and pastures—until the whole world looked like fairy land. Gretchen climbed up on a large stone which was beneath the window and carefully lifted down the wooden shoe. The snow tumbled off of it in a shower over the little girl's hands, but she did not heed that; she ran hurriedly back into the house, putting her hand into the toe of the shoe as she ran.

"Oh, Granny, Granny!" she exclaimed. "You did not believe the Christmas angels would think about us, but see, they have, they have! Here is a dear little bird nestled down in the toe of your shoe! Oh, isn't he beautiful?"

Granny came forward and looked at what the child was holding lovingly in her hand. There she saw a tiny chick-a-dee, whose wing was evidently broken by the rough and boisterous winds of the night before, and who had taken shelter in the safe, dry toe of the old wooden shoe. She gently took the little bird out of Gretchen's hands, and skilfully bound his broken wing to his side, so that he need not hurt himself trying to fly with it. Then she showed Gretchen how to make a nice warm nest for the little stranger, close beside the fire and when their breakfast was ready, she let Gretchen feed the little bird with a few moist crumbs.

Later in the day Gretchen carried the fresh, green boughs to the old sick man by the mill, and on her way home stopped to enjoy the Christmas toys of some other children that she knew, never once wishing they were hers. When she reached home she found that the little bird had gone to sleep. Soon, however, he opened his eyes and stretched his head up, saying just as plain as a bird can say: "Now, my new friends, I want you to give me something more to eat." Gretchen gladly fed him again, and then, holding him in her lap, she softly and gently stroked his gray feathers until the little creature seemed to lose all fear of her. That evening Granny taught her a Christmas hymn and told her another beautiful Christmas story. Then Gretchen made up a funny little story to tell the birdie. He winked his eyes and turned his head from side to side in such a droll fashion that Gretchen laughed until the tears came.

As Granny and she got ready for bed that night, Gretchen put her arms softly around Granny's neck, and whispered: "What a beautiful Christmas we have had today, Granny. Is there anything more lovely in all the world than Christmas?"

"Nay, child, nay," said Granny, "not to such loving hearts as yours."

THE THREE KINGS

Henry Wadsworth Longfellow

Three Kings came riding from far away,

Melchior and Gaspar and Baltasar;

Three Wise Men out of the East were they,

And they travelled by night and they slept by day,

For their guide was a beautiful, wonderful star.

The star was so beautiful, large and clear,

That all the other stars of the sky

Became a white mist in the atmosphere,

And by this they knew that the coming was near

Of the Prince foretold in the prophecy.

Three caskets they bore on their saddle-bows,
Three caskets of gold with golden keys;
Their robes were of crimson silk with rows
Of bells and pomegranates and furbelows,
Their turbans like blossoming almond-trees.

And so the Three Kings rode into the West,
Through the dusk of the night, over hill and dell,
And sometimes they nodded with beard on
    breast,
And sometimes talked, as they paused to rest,
With the people they met at some wayside well.

"Of the child that is born," said Baltasar,
"Good people, I pray you, tell us the news;
For we in the East have seen his star,
And have ridden fast, and have ridden far,
To find and worship the King of the Jews."

And the people answered, "You ask in vain;
We know of no King but Herod the Great!"
They thought the Wise Men were men insane,
As they spurred their horses across the plain,

Like riders in haste, who cannot wait.

And when they came to Jerusalem,
Herod the Great, who had heard this thing,
Sent for the Wise Men and questioned them;
And said, "Go down unto Bethlehem,
And bring me tidings of this new king."

So they rode away; and the star stood still,
The only one in the grey of morn;
Yes, it stopped—it stood still of its own free will,
Right over Bethlehem on the hill,
The city of David, where Christ was born.

And the Three Kings rode through the gate and
    the guard,
Through the silent street, till their horses turned
And neighed as they entered the great inn-yard;
But the windows were closed, and the doors were
    barred,
And only a light in the stable burned.

And cradled there in the scented hay,

In the air made sweet by the breath of kine,
The little child in the manger lay,
The child, that would be king one day
Of a kingdom not human, but divine.

His mother Mary of Nazareth
Sat watching beside his place of rest,
Watching the even flow of his breath,
For the joy of life and the terror of death
Were mingled together in her breast.

They laid their offerings at his feet:
The gold was their tribute to a King,
The frankincense, with its odor sweet,
Was for the Priest, the Paraclete,
The myrrh for the body's burying.

And the mother wondered and bowed her head,
And sat as still as a statue of stone,
Her heart was troubled yet comforted,
Remembering what the Angel had said
Of an endless reign and of David's throne.

Then the Kings rode out of the city gate,

With a clatter of hoofs in proud array;
But they went not back to Herod the Great,
For they knew his malice and feared his hate,
And returned to their homes by another way.

A Country Christmas

Louisa May Alcott

"A handful of good life is worth a bushel of learning."

"Dear Emily,—I have a brilliant idea, and at once hasten to share it with you. Three weeks ago I came up here to the wilds of Vermont to visit my old aunt, also to get a little quiet and distance in which to survey certain new prospects which have opened before me, and to decide whether I will marry a millionnaire and become a queen of society, or remain 'the charming Miss Vaughan' and wait till the conquering hero comes.

"Aunt Plumy begs me to stay over Christmas, and I

have consented, as I always dread the formal dinner with which my guardian celebrates the day.

"My brilliant idea is this. I'm going to make it a real old-fashioned frolic, and won't you come and help me? You will enjoy it immensely I am sure, for Aunt is a character, Cousin Saul worth seeing, and Ruth a far prettier girl than any of the city rose-buds coming out this season. Bring Leonard Randal along with you to take notes for his new books; then it will be fresher and truer than the last, clever as it was.

"The air is delicious up here, society amusing, this old farmhouse full of treasures, and your bosom friend pining to embrace you. Just telegraph yes or no, and we will expect you on Tuesday.

"Ever yours,

"SOPHIE VAUGHAN."

"They will both come, for they are as tired of city life and as fond of change as I am," said the writer of the above, as she folded her letter and went to get it posted without delay.

Aunt Plumy was in the great kitchen making pies; a jolly old soul, with a face as ruddy as a winter apple, a cheery voice, and the kindest heart that ever beat under a gingham gown. Pretty Ruth was chopping the mince, and singing so gaily as she worked that the four-and-twenty immortal blackbirds could not have put more music into a pie than she did. Saul was piling wood into the big oven, and Sophie paused a moment on the threshold to look at him, for she always enjoyed the sight of this stalwart cousin, whom she likened to a Norse viking, with his fair hair and beard, keen blue eyes, and six feet of manly height, with shoulders that looked broad and strong enough to bear any burden.

His back was toward her, but he saw her first, and turned his flushed face to meet her, with the sudden lighting up it always showed when she approached.

"I've done it, Aunt; and now I want Saul to post the letter, so we can get a speedy answer."

"Just as soon as I can hitch up, cousin"; and Saul pitched in his last log, looking ready to put a girdle round the earth in less than forty minutes.

"Well, dear, I ain't the least mite of objection, as long as it pleases you. I guess we can stan' it ef your city folks can. I presume to say things will look kind of sing'lar to 'em, but I s'pose that's what they come for. Idle folks do dreadful queer things to amuse 'em"; and Aunt Plumy leaned on the rolling-pin to smile and nod with a shrewd twinkle of her eye, as if she enjoyed the prospect as much as Sophie did.

"I shall be afraid of 'em, but I'll try not to make you ashamed of me," said Ruth, who loved her charming cousin even more than she admired her.

"No fear of that, dear. They will be the awkward ones, and you must set them at ease by just being your simple selves, and treating them as if they were every-day people. Nell is very nice and jolly when she drops her city ways, as she must here. She will enter into the spirit of the fun at once, and I know you'll all like her. Mr. Randal is rather the worse for too much praise and petting, as successful people are apt to be, so a little plain talk and rough work will do him good. He is a true gentleman in spite of his airs and elegance, and he will take it all in good part, if you treat him like a man and not a lion."

"I'll see to him," said Saul, who had listened with great interest to the latter part of Sophie's speech, evidently suspecting a lover, and enjoying the idea of supplying him with a liberal amount of "plain talk and rough work."

"I'll keep 'em busy if that's what they need, for there will be a sight to do, and we can't get help easy up here. Our darters don't hire out much. Work to home till they marry, and don't go gaddin' 'round gettin' their heads full of foolish notions, and forgettin' all the useful things their mothers taught 'em."

Aunt Plumy glanced at Ruth as she spoke, and a sudden color in the girl's cheeks proved that the words hit certain ambitious fancies of this pretty daughter of the house of Basset.

"They shall do their parts and not be a trouble; I'll see to that, for you certainly are the dearest aunt in the world to let me take possession of you and yours in this way," cried Sophie, embracing the old lady with warmth.

Saul wished the embrace could be returned by proxy, as his mother's hands were too floury to do more than hover affectionately round the delicate face that looked so fresh and young beside her wrinkled one. As it could not be done, he fled temptation and "hitched up" without delay.

The three women laid their heads together in his absence, and Sophie's plan grew apace, for Ruth longed to see a real novelist and a fine lady, and Aunt Plumy, having plans of her own to further, said "Yes, dear," to every suggestion.

Great was the arranging and adorning that went on that day in the old farmhouse, for Sophie wanted her friends to enjoy this taste of country pleasures, and knew just what additions would be indispensable to their comfort; what simple ornaments would be in keeping with the rustic stage on which she meant to play the part of prima donna.

Next day a telegram arrived accepting the invitation, for both the lady and the lion. They would arrive that afternoon, as little preparation was needed for this impromptu journey, the novelty of which was its chief charm to these blasé people.

Saul wanted to get out the double sleigh and span, for he prided himself on his horses, and a fall of snow came most opportunely to beautify the landscape and add a new pleasure to Christmas festivities.

But Sophie declared that the old yellow sleigh, with Punch, the farm-horse, must be used, as she wished everything to be in keeping; and Saul obeyed, thinking he had never seen anything prettier than his cousin when she appeared in his mother's old-fashioned camlet cloak and blue silk pumpkin hood. He looked remarkably well himself in his fur coat, with hair and beard brushed till they shone like spun gold, a fresh color in his cheek, and the sparkle of amusement in his eyes, while excitement gave his usually grave face the animation it needed to be handsome.

Away they jogged in the creaking old sleigh, leaving Ruth to make herself pretty, with a fluttering heart, and Aunt Plumy to dish up a late dinner fit to tempt the most fastidious appetite.

"She has not come for us, and there is not even a stage to take us up. There must be some mistake," said Emily Herrick, as she looked about the shabby little station where they were set down.

"That is the never-to-be-forgotten face of our fair friend, but the bonnet of her grandmother, if my eyes do not deceive me," answered Randal, turning to survey the couple approaching in the rear.

"Sophie Vaughan, what do you mean by making such a guy of yourself?" exclaimed Emily, as she kissed the smiling face in the hood and stared at the quaint cloak.

"I'm dressed for my part, and I intend to keep it up. This is our host, my cousin, Saul Basset. Come to the sleigh at once, he will see to your luggage," said Sophie, painfully conscious of the antiquity of her array as her eyes rested on Emily's pretty hat and mantle, and the masculine elegance of Randal's wraps.

They were hardly tucked in when Saul appeared with a valise in one hand and a large trunk on his shoulder, swinging both on to a wood-sled that stood near by as easily as if they had been hand-bags.

"That is your hero, is it? Well, he looks it, calm and comely, taciturn and tall," said Emily, in a tone of approbation.

"He should have been named Samson or Goliath; though I believe it was the small man who slung things about and turned out the hero in the end," added Randal, surveying the performance with interest and a touch of envy, for much pen work had made his own hands as delicate as a woman's.

"Saul doesn't live in a glass house, so stones won't hurt him. Remember sarcasm is forbidden and sincerity the order of the day. You are country folks now, and it will do you good to try their simple, honest ways for a few days."

Sophie had no time to say more, for Saul came up and drove off with the brief remark that the baggage would "be along right away."

Being hungry, cold and tired, the guests were rather silent during the short drive, but Aunt Plumy's hospitable welcome, and the savory fumes of the dinner awaiting them, thawed the ice and won their hearts at once.

"Isn't it nice? Aren't you glad you came?" asked Sophie, as she led her friends into the parlor, which she had redeemed from its primness by putting bright chintz curtains to the windows, hemlock boughs over the old portraits, a china bowl of flowers on the table, and a splendid fire on the wide hearth.

"It is perfectly jolly, and this is the way I begin to enjoy myself," answered Emily, sitting down upon the home-made rug, whose red flannel roses bloomed in a blue list basket.

"If I may add a little smoke to your glorious fire, it will be quite perfect. Won't Samson join me?" asked Randal, waiting for permission, cigar-case in hand.

"He has no small vices, but you may indulge yours," answered Sophie, from the depths of a grandmotherly chair.

Emily glanced up at her friend as if she caught a new tone in her voice, then turned to the fire again with a wise little nod, as if confiding some secret to the reflection of herself in the bright brass andiron.

"His Delilah does not take this form. I wait with interest to discover if he has one. What a daisy the sister is. Does she ever speak?" asked Randal, trying to lounge on the haircloth sofa, where he was slipping uncomfortably about.

"Oh yes, and sings like a bird. You shall hear her when she gets over her shyness. But no trifling, mind you, for it is a jealously guarded daisy and not to be picked by any idle hand," said Sophie warningly, as she recalled Ruth's blushes and Randal's compliments at dinner.

"I should expect to be annihilated by the big brother if I attempted any but the 'sincerest' admiration and respect. Have no fears on that score, but tell us what is to follow this superb dinner. An apple bee, spinning match, husking party, or primitive pastime of some sort, I have no doubt."

"As you are new to our ways I am going to let you rest this evening. We will sit about the fire and tell stories. Aunt is a master hand at that, and Saul has reminiscences of the war that are well worth hearing if we can only get him to tell them."

"Ah, he was there, was he?"

"Yes, all through it, and is Major Basset, though he likes his plain name best. He fought splendidly and had several wounds, though only a mere boy when he earned his scars and bars. I'm very proud of him for that," and Sophie looked so as she glanced at the photograph of a stripling in uniform set in the place of honor on the high mantel-piece.

"We must stir him up and hear these martial memories. I want some new incidents, and shall book all I can get, if I may."

Here Randal was interrupted by Saul himself, who came in with an armful of wood for the fire.

"Anything more I can do for you, cousin?" he asked, surveying the scene with a rather wistful look.

"Only come and sit with us and talk over war times with Mr. Randal."

"When I've foddered the cattle and done my chores

I'd be pleased to. What regiment were you in?" asked Saul, looking down from his lofty height upon the slender gentleman, who answered briefly,—

"In none. I was abroad at the time."

"Sick?"

"No, busy with a novel."

"Took four years to write it?"

"I was obliged to travel and study before I could finish it. These things take more time to work up than outsiders would believe."

"Seems to me our war was a finer story than any you could find in Europe, and the best way to study it would be to fight it out. If you want heroes and heroines you'd have found plenty of 'em there."

"I have no doubt of it, and shall be glad to atone for my seeming neglect of them by hearing about your own exploits, Major."

Randal hoped to turn the conversation gracefully, but Saul was not to be caught, and left the room, saying, with a gleam of fun in his eye,—

"I can't stop now; heroes can wait, pigs can't."

The girls laughed at this sudden descent from the sublime to the ridiculous, and Randal joined them, feeling his condescension had not been unobserved.

As if drawn by the merry sound Aunt Plumy appeared, and being established in the rocking-chair fell to talking as easily as if she had known her guests for years.

"Laugh away, young folks, that's better for digestion than any of the messes people use. Are you troubled with dyspepsy, dear? You didn't seem to take your vittles very hearty, so I mistrusted you was delicate," she said, looking at Emily, whose pale cheeks and weary eyes told the story of late hours and a gay life.

"I haven't eaten so much for years, I assure you, Mrs. Basset; but it was impossible to taste all your good things. I am not dyspeptic, thank you, but a little seedy and tired, for I've been working rather hard lately."

"Be you a teacher? or have you a 'perfessun,' as they call a trade nowadays?" asked the old lady in a tone of kindly interest, which prevented a laugh at the idea of Emily's being anything but a beauty and a belle. The others kept their countenances with difficulty, and she answered demurely,—

"I have no trade as yet, but I dare say I should be happier if I had."

"Not a doubt on't, my dear."

"What would you recommend, ma'am?"

"I should say dressmakin' was rather in your line, ain't it? Your clothes is dreadful tasty, and do you credit if you made 'em yourself," and Aunt Plumy surveyed with feminine interest the simple elegance of the travelling dress which was the masterpiece of a French modiste.

"No, ma'am, I don't make my own things, I'm too lazy. It takes so much time and trouble to select them that I have only strength left to wear them."

"Housekeepin' used to be the favorite perfessun in my day. It ain't fashionable now, but it needs a sight of trainin' to be perfect in all that's required, and I've an idee it would be a sight healthier and usefuller than the paintin' and music and fancy work young women do nowadays."

"But every one wants some beauty in their lives, and each one has a different sphere to fill, if one can only find it."

"'Pears to me there's no call for so much art when nater is full of beauty for them that can see and love it. As for 'spears' and so on, I've a notion if each of us did up our own little chores smart and thorough we needn't go wanderin' round to set the world to rights. That's the Lord's job, and I presume to say He can do it without any advice of ourn."

Something in the homely but true words seemed to rebuke the three listeners for wasted lives, and for a moment there was no sound but the crackle of the fire, the brisk click of the old lady's knitting needles, and Ruth's voice singing overhead as she made ready to join the party below.

"To judge by that sweet sound you have done one of your 'chores' very beautifully, Mrs. Basset, and in spite of the follies of our day, succeeded in keeping one girl healthy, happy and unspoiled," said Emily, looking up into the peaceful old face with her own lovely one full of respect and envy.

"I do hope so, for she's my ewe lamb, the last of four dear little girls; all the rest are in the burying ground 'side of father. I don't expect to keep her long, and don't ought to regret when I lose her, for Saul is the best of sons; but daughters is more to mothers somehow, and I always yearn over girls that is left without a broodin' wing to keep 'em safe and warm in this world of tribulation."

Aunt Plumy laid her hand on Sophie's head as she spoke, with such a motherly look that both girls drew nearer, and Randal resolved to put her in a book without delay.

Presently Saul returned with little Ruth hanging on his arm and shyly nestling near him as he took the three-cornered leathern chair in the chimney nook, while she sat on a stool close by.

"Now the circle is complete and the picture perfect. Don't light the lamps yet, please, but talk away and let me make a mental study of you. I seldom find so charming a scene to paint," said Randal, beginning to enjoy himself immensely, with a true artist's taste for novelty and effect.

"Tell us about your book, for we have been reading it as it comes out in the magazine, and are much exercised about how it's going to end," began Saul, gallantly throwing himself into the breach, for a momentary embarrassment fell upon the women at the idea of sitting for their portraits before they were ready.

"Do you really read my poor serial up here, and do me the honor to like it?" asked the novelist, both flattered and amused, for his work was of the aesthetic sort, microscopic studies of character, and careful pictures of modern life.

"Sakes alive, why shouldn't we," cried Aunt Plumy. "We have some eddication, though we ain't very genteel. We've got a town libry, kep up by the women mostly, with fairs and tea parties and so on. We have all the magazines reg'lar, and Saul reads out the pieces while Ruth sews and I knit, my eyes bein' poor. Our winter is long and evenins would be kinder lonesome if we didn't have novils and newspapers to cheer 'em up."

"I am very glad I can help to beguile them for you. Now tell me what you honestly think of my work? Criticism is always valuable, and I should really like yours, Mrs. Basset," said Randal, wondering what the good woman would make of the delicate analysis and worldly wisdom on which he prided himself.

Short work, as Aunt Plumy soon showed him, for she rather enjoyed freeing her mind at all times, and decidedly resented the insinuation that country folk could not appreciate light literature as well as city people.

"I ain't no great of a jedge about anything but nat'ralness of books, and it really does seem as if some of your men and women was dreadful uncomfortable creaters. 'Pears to me it ain't wise to be always pickin' ourselves to pieces and pryin' into things that ought to come gradual by way of experience and the visitations of Providence. Flowers won't blow worth a cent ef you pull 'em open. Better wait and see what they can do alone. I do relish the smart sayins, the odd ways of furrin parts, and the sarcastic slaps at folkses weak spots. But, massy knows, we can't live on spice-cake and Charlotte Ruche, and I do feel as if books was more sustainin' ef they was full of every-day people and things, like good bread and butter. Them that goes to the heart and ain't soon forgotten is the kind I hanker for. Mis Terry's books now, and Mis Stowe's, and Dickens's Christmas pieces,—them is real sweet and cheerin', to my mind."

As the blunt old lady paused it was evident she had produced a sensation, for Saul smiled at the fire, Ruth looked dismayed at this assault upon one of her idols, and the young ladies were both astonished and amused at the keenness of the new critic who dared express what they had often felt. Randal, however, was quite composed and laughed good-naturedly, though secretly feeling as if a pail of cold water had been poured over him.

"Many thanks, madam; you have discovered my weak point with surprising accuracy. But you see I cannot help 'picking folks to pieces,' as you have expressed it; that is my gift, and it has its attractions, as the sale of my books will testify. People like the 'spice-bread,' and as that is the only sort my oven will bake, I must keep on in order to make my living."

"So rumsellers say, but it ain't a good trade to foller, and I'd chop wood 'fore I'd earn my livin' harmin' my feller man. 'Pears to me I'd let my oven cool a spell, and hunt up some homely, happy folks to write about; folks that don't borrer trouble and go lookin' for holes in their neighbors' coats, but take their lives brave and cheerful; and rememberin' we are all human, have pity on the weak, and try to be as full of mercy, patience and lovin' kindness as Him who made us. That sort of a book would do a heap of good; be real warmin' and strengthenin', and make them that read it love the man that wrote it, and remember him when he was dead and gone."

"I wish I could!" and Randal meant what he said, for he was as tired of his own style, as a watch-maker might be of the magnifying glass through which he strains his eyes all day. He knew that the heart was left out of his work, and that both mind and soul were growing morbid with dwelling on the faulty, absurd and metaphysical phases of life and character. He often threw down his pen and vowed he would write no more; but he loved ease and the books brought money readily; he was accustomed to the stimulant of praise and missed it as the toper misses his wine, so that which had once been a pleasure to himself and others was fast becoming a burden and a disappointment.

The brief pause which followed his involuntary betrayal of discontent was broken by Ruth, who exclaimed, with a girlish enthusiasm that overpowered girlish bashfulness,—

"I think all the novels are splendid! I hope you will write hundreds more, and I shall live to read 'em."

"Bravo, my gentle champion! I promise that I will write one more at least, and have a heroine in it whom your mother will both admire and love," answered Randal, surprised to find how grateful he was for the girl's approval, and how rapidly his trained fancy began to paint the background on which he hoped to copy this fresh, human daisy.

Abashed by her involuntary outburst, Ruth tried to efface herself behind Saul's broad shoulder, and he brought the conversation back to its starting-point by saying in a tone of the most sincere interest,—

"Speaking of the serial, I am very anxious to know how your hero comes out. He is a fine fellow, and I can't decide whether he is going to spoil his life marrying that silly woman, or do something grand and generous, and not be made a fool of."

"Upon my soul, I don't know myself. It is very hard to find new finales. Can't you suggest something, Major? then I shall not be obliged to leave my story without an end, as people complain I am rather fond of doing."

"Well, no, I don't think I've anything to offer. Seems to me it isn't the sensational exploits that show the hero best, but some great sacrifice quietly made by a common sort of man who is noble without knowing it. I saw a good many such during the war, and often wish I could write them down, for it is surprising how much courage, goodness and real piety is stowed away in common folks ready to show when the right time comes."

"Tell us one of them, and I'll bless you for a hint. No one knows the anguish of an author's spirit when he can't ring down the curtain on an effective tableau," said Randal, with a glance at his friends to ask their aid in eliciting an anecdote or reminiscence.

"Tell about the splendid fellow who held the bridge, like Horatius, till help came up. That was a thrilling story, I assure you," answered Sophie, with an inviting smile.

But Saul would not be his own hero, and said briefly:

"Any man can be brave when the battle-fever is on him, and it only takes a little physical courage to dash ahead." He paused a moment, with his eyes on the snowy landscape without, where twilight was deepening; then, as if constrained by the memory that winter scene evoked, he slowly continued,—

"One of the bravest things I ever knew was done by a poor fellow who has been a hero to me ever since, though I only met him that night. It was after one of the big battles of that last winter, and I was knocked over with a broken leg and two or three bullets here and there. Night was coming on, snow falling, and a sharp wind blew over the field where a lot of us lay, dead and alive, waiting for the ambulance to come and pick us up. There was skirmishing going on not far off, and our prospects were rather poor between frost and fire. I was calculating how I'd manage, when I found two poor chaps close by who were worse off, so I braced up and did what I could for them. One had an arm blown away, and kept up a dreadful groaning. The other was shot bad, and bleeding to death for want of help, but never complained. He was nearest, and I liked his pluck, for he spoke cheerful and made me ashamed to growl. Such times make dreadful brutes of men if they haven't something to hold on to, and all three of us were most wild with pain and cold and hunger, for we'd fought all day fasting, when we heard a rumble in the road below, and saw lanterns bobbing round. That meant life to us, and we all tried to holler; two of us were pretty faint, but I managed a good yell, and they heard it.

"'Room for one more. Hard luck, old boys, but we are full and must save the worst wounded first. Take a drink, and hold on till we come back,' says one of them with the stretcher.

"'Here's the one to go,' I says, pointin' out my man, for I saw by the light that he was hard hit.

"'No, that one. He's got more chances than I, or this one; he's young and got a mother; I'll wait,' said the good feller, touchin' my arm, for he'd heard me mutterin' to myself about this dear old lady. We always want mother when we are down, you know."

Saul's eyes turned to the beloved face with a glance of tenderest affection, and Aunt Plumy answered with a dismal groan at the recollection of his need that night, and her absence.

"Well, to be short, the groaning chap was taken, and my man left. I was mad, but there was no time for talk, and the selfish one went off and left that poor feller to run his one chance. I had my rifle, and guessed I could hobble up to use it if need be; so we settled back to wait without much hope of help, everything being in a muddle. And wait we did till morning, for that ambulance did not come back till next day, when most of us were past needing it.

"I'll never forget that night. I dream it all over again as plain as if it was real. Snow, cold, darkness, hunger, thirst, pain, and all round us cries and cursing growing less and less, till at last only the wind went moaning over that meadow. It was awful! so lonesome, helpless, and seemingly God-forsaken. Hour after hour we lay there side by side under one coat, waiting to be saved or die, for the wind grew strong and we grew weak."

Saul drew a long breath, and held his hands to the fire as if he felt again the sharp suffering of that night.

"And the man?" asked Emily, softly, as if reluctant to break the silence.

"He was a man! In times like that men talk like brothers and show what they are. Lying there, slowly freezing, Joe

Cummings told me about his wife and babies, his old folks waiting for him, all depending on him, yet all ready to give him up when he was needed. A plain man, but honest and true, and loving as a woman; I soon saw that as he went on talking, half to me and half to himself, for sometimes he wandered a little toward the end. I've read books, heard sermons, and seen good folks, but nothing ever came so close or did me so much good as seeing this man die. He had one chance and gave it cheerfully. He longed for those he loved, and let 'em go with a good-by they couldn't hear. He suffered all the pains we most shrink from without a murmur, and kept my heart warm while his own was growing cold. It's no use trying to tell that part of it; but I heard prayers that night that meant something, and I saw how faith could hold a soul up when everything was gone but God."

Saul stopped there with a sudden huskiness in his deep voice, and when he went on it was in the tone of one who speaks of a dear friend.

"Joe grew still by and by, and I thought he was asleep, for I felt his breath when I tucked him up, and his hand held on to mine. The cold sort of numbed me, and I dropped off, too weak and stupid to think or feel. I never should have waked up if it hadn't been for Joe. When I came to, it was morning, and I thought I was dead, for all I could see was that great field of white mounds, like graves, and a splendid sky above. Then I looked for Joe, remembering; but he had put my coat back over me, and lay stiff and still under the snow that covered him like a shroud, all except his face. A bit of my cape had blown over it, and when I took it off and the sun shone on his dead face, I declare to you it was so full of heavenly peace I felt as if that common man had been glorified by God's light, and rewarded by God's 'Well done.' That's all."

No one spoke for a moment, while the women wiped their eyes, and Saul dropped his as if to hide something softer than tears.

"It was very noble, very touching. And you? how did you get off at last?" asked Randal, with real admiration and respect in his usually languid face.

"Crawled off," answered Saul, relapsing into his former brevity of speech.

"Why not before, and save yourself all that misery?"

"Couldn't leave Joe."

"Ah, I see; there were two heroes that night."

"Dozens, I've no doubt. Those were times that made heroes of men, and women, too."

"Tell us more"; begged Emily, looking up with an expression none of her admirers ever brought to her face by their softest compliments or wiliest gossip.

"I've done my part. It's Mr. Randal's turn now"; and Saul drew himself out of the ruddy circle of firelight, as if ashamed of the prominent part he was playing.

Sophie and her friend had often heard Randal talk, for he was an accomplished raconteur, but that night he exerted himself, and was unusually brilliant and entertaining, as if upon his mettle. The Bassets were charmed. They sat late and were very merry, for Aunt Plumy got up a little supper for them, and her cider was as exhilarating as champagne. When they parted for the night and Sophie kissed her aunt, Emily did the same, saying heartily,—

"It seems as if I'd known you all my life, and this is certainly the most enchanting old place that ever was."

"Glad you like it, dear. But it ain't all fun, as you'll find out to-morrow when you go to work, for Sophie says you must," answered Mrs. Basset, as her guests trooped away, rashly promising to like everything.

They found it difficult to keep their word when they were called at half past six next morning. Their rooms were warm, however, and they managed to scramble down in time for breakfast, guided by the fragrance of coffee and Aunt Plumy's shrill voice singing the good old hymn—

"Lord, in the morning Thou shalt hear
My voice ascending high."

An open fire blazed on the hearth, for the cooking was done in the lean-to, and the spacious, sunny kitchen was kept in all its old-fashioned perfection, with the wooden settle in a warm nook, the tall clock behind the door, copper and pewter utensils shining on the dresser, old china in the corner closet and a little spinning wheel rescued from the garret by Sophie to adorn the deep window, full of scarlet geraniums, Christmas roses, and white chrysanthemums.

The young lady, in a checked apron and mob-cap, greeted her friends with a dish of buckwheats in one hand, and a pair of cheeks that proved she had been learning to fry these delectable cakes.

"You do 'keep it up' in earnest, upon my word; and very becoming it is, dear. But won't you ruin your complexion and roughen your hands if you do so much of this new fancy-work?" asked Emily, much amazed at this novel freak.

"I like it, and really believe I've found my proper sphere at last. Domestic life seems so pleasant to me that I feel as if I'd better keep it up for the rest of my life," answered Sophie, making a pretty picture of herself as she cut great slices of brown bread, with the early sunshine touching her happy face.

"The charming Miss Vaughan in the role of a farmer's wife. I find it difficult to imagine, and shrink from the thought of the wide-spread dismay such a fate will produce among her adorers," added Randal, as he basked in the glow of the hospitable fire.

"She might do worse; but come to breakfast and do honor to my handiwork," said Sophie, thinking of her worn-out millionnaire, and rather nettled by the satiric smile on Randal's lips.

"What an appetite early rising gives one. I feel equal to almost anything, so let me help wash cups," said Emily, with unusual energy, when the hearty meal was over and Sophie began to pick up the dishes as if it was her usual work.

Ruth went to the window to water the flowers, and Randal followed to make himself agreeable, remembering her defence of him last night. He was used to admiration from feminine eyes, and flattery from soft lips, but found something new and charming in the innocent delight which showed itself at his approach in blushes more eloquent than words, and shy glances from eyes full of hero-worship.

"I hope you are going to spare me a posy for tomorrow night, since I can be fine in no other way to do honor to the dance Miss Sophie proposes for us," he said, leaning in the bay window to look down on the little girl, with the devoted air he usually wore for pretty women.

"Anything you like! I should be so glad to have you wear my flowers. There will be enough for all, and I've nothing else to give to people who have made me as happy as cousin Sophie and you," answered Ruth, half drowning her great calla as she spoke with grateful warmth.

"You must make her happy by accepting the invitation to go home with her which I heard given last night. A peep at the world would do you good, and be a pleasant change, I think."

"Oh, very pleasant! but would it do me good?" and Ruth looked up with sudden seriousness in her blue eyes, as a child questions an elder, eager, yet wistful.

"Why not?" asked Randal, wondering at the hesitation.

"I might grow discontented with things here if I saw splendid houses and fine people. I am very happy now, and it would break my heart to lose that happiness, or ever learn to be ashamed of home."

"But don't you long for more pleasure, new scenes and other friends than these?" asked the man, touched by the little creature's loyalty to the things she knew and loved.

"Very often, but mother says when I'm ready they will come, so I wait and try not to be impatient." But Ruth's eyes looked out over the green leaves as if the longing was very strong within her to see more of the unknown world lying beyond the mountains that hemmed her in.

"It is natural for birds to hop out of the nest, so I shall expect to see you over there before long, and ask you how you enjoy your first flight," said Randal, in a paternal tone that had a curious effect on Ruth.

To his surprise, she laughed, then blushed like one of her own roses, and answered with a demure dignity that was very pretty to see.

"I intend to hop soon, but it won't be a very long flight or very far from mother. She can't spare me, and nobody in the world can fill her place to me."

"Bless the child, does she think I'm going to make love to her," thought Randal, much amused, but quite mistaken. Wiser women had thought so when he assumed the caressing air with which he beguiled them into the little revelations of character he liked to use, as the south wind makes flowers open their hearts to give up their odor, then leaves them to carry it elsewhere, the more welcome for the stolen sweetness.

"Perhaps you are right. The maternal wing is a safe shelter for confiding little souls like you, Miss Ruth. You will be as comfortable here as your flowers in this sunny window," he said, carelessly pinching geranium leaves, and ruffling the roses till the pink petals of the largest fluttered to the floor.

As if she instinctively felt and resented something in the man which his act symbolized, the girl answered quietly, as she went on with her work, "Yes, if the frost does not touch me, or careless people spoil me too soon."

Before Randal could reply Aunt Plumy approached like a maternal hen who sees her chicken in danger.

"Saul is goin' to haul wood after he's done his chores, mebbe you'd like to go along? The view is good, the roads well broke, and the day uncommon fine."

"Thanks; it will be delightful, I dare say," politely responded the lion, with a secret shudder at the idea of a rural promenade at 8 a.m. in the winter.

"Come on, then; we'll feed the stock, and then I'll show you how to yoke oxen," said Saul, with a twinkle in his eye as he led the way, when his new aide had muffled himself up as if for a polar voyage.

"Now, that's too bad of Saul! He did it on purpose, just to please you, Sophie," cried Ruth presently, and the girls ran to the window to behold Randal bravely following his host with a pail of pigs' food in each hand, and an expression of resigned disgust upon his aristocratic face.

"To what base uses may we come," quoted Emily, as

they all nodded and smiled upon the victim as he looked back from the barn-yard, where he was clamorously welcomed by his new charges.

"It is rather a shock at first, but it will do him good, and Saul won't be too hard upon him, I'm sure," said Sophie, going back to her work, while Ruth turned her best buds to the sun that they might be ready for a peace-offering to-morrow.

There was a merry clatter in the big kitchen for an hour; then Aunt Plumy and her daughter shut themselves up in the pantry to perform some culinary rites, and the young ladies went to inspect certain antique costumes laid forth in Sophie's room.

"You see, Em, I thought it would be appropriate to the house and season to have an old-fashioned dance. Aunt has quantities of ancient finery stowed away, for great-grandfather Basset was a fine old gentleman and his family lived in state. Take your choice of the crimson, blue or silver-gray damask. Ruth is to wear the worked muslin and quilted white satin skirt, with that coquettish hat."

"Being dark, I'll take the red and trim it up with this fine lace. You must wear the blue and primrose, with the distracting high-heeled shoes. Have you any suits for the men?" asked Emily, throwing herself at once into the all-absorbing matter of costume.

"A claret velvet coat and vest, silk stockings, cocked hat and snuff-box for Randal. Nothing large enough for Saul, so he must wear his uniform. Won't Aunt Plumy be superb in this plum-colored satin and immense cap?"

A delightful morning was spent in adapting the faded finery of the past to the blooming beauty of the present, and time and tongues flew till the toot of a horn called them down to dinner.

The girls were amazed to see Randal come whistling up the road with his trousers tucked into his boots, blue mittens on his hands, and an unusual amount of energy in his whole figure, as he drove the oxen, while Saul laughed at his vain attempts to guide the bewildered beasts.

"It's immense! The view from the hill is well worth seeing, for the snow glorifies the landscape and reminds one of Switzerland. I'm going to make a sketch of it this afternoon; better come and enjoy the delicious freshness, young ladies."

Randal was eating with such an appetite that he did not see the glances the girls exchanged as they promised to go.

"Bring home some more winter-green, I want things to be real nice, and we haven't enough for the kitchen," said Ruth, dimpling with girlish delight as she imagined herself dancing under the green garlands in her grandmother's wedding gown.

It was very lovely on the hill, for far as the eye could reach lay the wintry landscape sparkling with the brief beauty of sunshine on virgin snow. Pines sighed overhead, hardy birds flitted to and fro, and in all the trodden spots rose the little spires of evergreen ready for its Christmas duty. Deeper in the wood sounded the measured ring of axes, the crash of falling trees, while the red shirts of the men added color to the scene, and a fresh wind brought the aromatic breath of newly cloven hemlock and pine.

"How beautiful it is! I never knew before what winter woods were like. Did you, Sophie?" asked Emily, sitting on a stump to enjoy the novel pleasure at her ease.

"I've found out lately; Saul lets me come as often as I like, and this fine air seems to make a new creature of me," answered Sophie, looking about her with sparkling eyes, as if this was a kingdom where she reigned supreme.

"Something is making a new creature of you, that is very evident. I haven't yet discovered whether it is the air or some magic herb among that green stuff you are gathering so diligently"; and Emily laughed to see the color deepen beautifully in her friend's half-averted face.

"Scarlet is the only wear just now, I find. If we are lost

like babes in the woods there are plenty of redbreasts to cover us with leaves," and Randal joined Emily's laugh, with a glance at Saul, who had just pulled his coat off.

"You wanted to see this tree go down, so stand from under and I'll show you how it's done," said the farmer, taking up his axe, not unwilling to gratify his guests and display his manly accomplishments at the same time.

It was a fine sight, the stalwart man swinging his axe with magnificent strength and skill, each blow sending a thrill through the stately tree, till its heart was reached and it tottered to its fall. Never pausing for breath Saul shook his yellow mane out of his eyes, and hewed away, while the drops stood on his forehead and his arm ached, as bent on distinguishing himself as if he had been a knight tilting against his rival for his lady's favor.

"I don't know which to admire most, the man or his muscle. One doesn't often see such vigor, size and comeliness in these degenerate days," said Randal, mentally booking the fine figure in the red shirt.

"I think we have discovered a rough diamond. I only wonder if Sophie is going to try and polish it," answered Emily, glancing at her friend, who stood a little apart, watching the rise and fall of the axe as intently as if her fate depended on it.

Down rushed the tree at last, and, leaving them to examine a crow's nest in its branches, Saul went off to his men, as if he found the praises of his prowess rather too much for him.

Randal fell to sketching, the girls to their garland-making, and for a little while the sunny woodland nook was full of lively chat and pleasant laughter, for the air exhilarated them all like wine. Suddenly a man came running from the wood, pale and anxious, saying, as he hastened by for help, "Blasted tree fell on him! Bleed to death before the doctor comes!"

"Who? who?" cried the startled trio.

But the man ran on, with some breathless reply, in which only a name was audible—"Basset."

"The deuce it is!" and Randal dropped his pencil, while the girls sprang up in dismay. Then, with one impulse, they hastened to the distant group, half visible behind the fallen trees and corded wood.

Sophie was there first, and forcing her way through the little crowd of men, saw a red-shirted figure on the ground, crushed and bleeding, and threw herself down beside it with a cry that pierced the hearts of those who heard it.

In the act she saw it was not Saul, and covered her bewildered face as if to hide its joy. A strong arm lifted her, and the familiar voice said cheeringly,—

"I'm all right, dear. Poor Bruce is hurt, but we've sent for help. Better go right home and forget all about it."

"Yes, I will, if I can do nothing"; and Sophie meekly returned to her friends who stood outside the circle over which Saul's head towered, assuring them of his safety.

Hoping they had not seen her agitation, she led Emily away, leaving Randal to give what aid he could and bring them news of the poor wood-chopper's state.

Aunt Plumy produced the "camphire" the moment she saw Sophie's pale face, and made her lie down, while the brave old lady trudged briskly off with bandages and brandy to the scene of action. On her return she brought comfortable news of the man, so the little flurry blew over and was forgotten by all but Sophie, who remained pale and quiet all the evening, tying evergreen as if her life depended on it.

"A good night's sleep will set her up. She ain't used to such things, dear child, and needs cossetin'," said Aunt Plumy, purring over her until she was in her bed, with a hot stone at her feet and a bowl of herb tea to quiet her nerves.

An hour later when Emily went up, she peeped in to see if Sophie was sleeping nicely, and was surprised to find the invalid wrapped in a dressing-gown writing busily.

"Last will and testament, or sudden inspiration, dear?

How are you? faint or feverish, delirious or in the dumps! Saul looks so anxious, and Mrs. Basset hushes us all up so, I came to bed, leaving Randal to entertain Ruth."

As she spoke Emily saw the papers disappear in a portfolio, and Sophie rose with a yawn.

"I was writing letters, but I'm sleepy now. Quite over my foolish fright, thank you. Go and get your beauty sleep that you may dazzle the natives to-morrow."

"So glad, good night"; and Emily went away, saying to herself, "Something is going on, and I must find out what it is before I leave. Sophie can't blind me."

But Sophie did all the next day, being delightfully gay at the dinner, and devoting herself to the young minister who was invited to meet the distinguished novelist, and evidently being afraid of him, gladly basked in the smiles of his charming neighbor. A dashing sleigh-ride occupied the afternoon, and then great was the fun and excitement over the costumes.

Aunt Plumy laughed till the tears rolled down her cheeks as the girls compressed her into the plum-colored gown with its short waist, leg-of-mutton sleeves, and narrow skirt. But a worked scarf hid all deficiencies, and the towering cap struck awe into the soul of the most frivolous observer.

"Keep an eye on me, girls, for I shall certainly split somewheres or lose my head-piece off when I'm trottin' round. What would my blessed mother say if she could see me rigged out in her best things?" and with a smile and a sigh the old lady departed to look after "the boys," and see that the supper was all right.

Three prettier damsels never tripped down the wide staircase than the brilliant brunette in crimson brocade, the pensive blonde in blue, or the rosy little bride in old muslin and white satin.

A gallant court gentleman met them in the hall with a superb bow, and escorted them to the parlor, where Grandma Basset's ghost was discovered dancing with a modern major in full uniform.

Mutual admiration and many compliments followed, till other ancient ladies and gentlemen arrived in all manner of queer costumes, and the old house seemed to wake from its humdrum quietude to sudden music and merriment, as if a past generation had returned to keep its Christmas there.

The village fiddler soon struck up the good old tunes, and then the strangers saw dancing that filled them with mingled mirth and envy; it was so droll, yet so hearty. The young men, unusually awkward in their grandfathers' knee-breeches, flapping vests, and swallow-tail coats, footed it bravely with the buxom girls who were the prettier for their quaintness, and danced with such vigor that their high combs stood awry, their furbelows waved wildly, and their cheeks were as red as their breast-knots, or hose.

It was impossible to stand still, and one after the other the city folk yielded to the spell, Randal leading off with Ruth, Sophie swept away by Saul, and Emily being taken possession of by a young giant of eighteen, who spun her around with a boyish impetuosity that took her breath away. Even Aunt Plumy was discovered jigging it alone in the pantry, as if the music was too much for her, and the plates and glasses jingled gaily on the shelves in time to Money Musk and Fishers' Hornpipe.

A pause came at last, however, and fans fluttered, heated brows were wiped, jokes were made, lovers exchanged confidences, and every nook and corner held a man and maid carrying on the sweet game which is never out of fashion. There was a glitter of gold lace in the back entry, and a train of blue and primrose shone in the dim light. There was a richer crimson than that of the geraniums in the deep window, and a dainty shoe tapped the bare floor impatiently as the brilliant black eyes looked everywhere for the court gentleman, while their owner listened to the gruff prattle of an enamored boy. But in the upper hall walked a little white ghost as if waiting for some shadowy companion, and when a dark form appeared ran to take its arm, saying, in a tone of soft satisfaction,—

"I was so afraid you wouldn't come!"

"Why did you leave me, Ruth?" answered a manly voice in a tone of surprise, though the small hand slipping from the velvet coat-sleeve was replaced as if it was pleasant to feel it there.

A pause, and then the other voice answered demurely,—

"Because I was afraid my head would be turned by the fine things you were saying."

"It is impossible to help saying what one feels to such an artless little creature as you are. It does me good to admire anything so fresh and sweet, and won't harm you."

"It might if—"

"If what, my daisy?"

"I believed it," and a laugh seemed to finish the broken sentence better than the words.

"You may, Ruth, for I do sincerely admire the most genuine girl I have seen for a long time. And walking here with you in your bridal white I was just asking myself if I should not be a happier man with a home of my own and a little wife hanging on my arm than drifting about the world as I do now with only myself to care for."

"I know you would!" and Ruth spoke so earnestly that Randal was both touched and startled, fearing he had ventured too far in a mood of unwonted sentiment, born of the romance of the hour and the sweet frankness of his companion.

"Then you don't think it would be rash for some sweet woman to take me in hand and make me happy, since fame is a failure?"

"Oh, no; it would be easy work if she loved you. I know some one—if I only dared to tell her name."

"Upon my soul, this is cool," and Randal looked down, wondering if the audacious lady on his arm could be shy Ruth.

If he had seen the malicious merriment in her eyes he would have been more humiliated still, but they were modestly averted, and the face under the little hat was full of a soft agitation rather dangerous even to a man of the world.

"She is a captivating little creature, but it is too soon for anything but a mild flirtation. I must delay further innocent revelations or I shall do something rash."

While making this excellent resolution Randal had been pressing the hand upon his arm and gently pacing down the dimly lighted hall with the sound of music in his ears,

Ruth's sweetest roses in his button-hole, and a loving little girl beside him, as he thought.

"You shall tell me by and by when we are in town. I am sure you will come, and meanwhile don't forget me."

"I am going in the spring, but I shall not be with Sophie," answered Ruth, in a whisper.

"With whom then? I shall long to see you."

"With my husband. I am to be married in May."

"The deuce you are!" escaped Randal, as he stopped short to stare at his companion, sure she was not in earnest.

But she was, for as he looked the sound of steps coming up the back stairs made her whole face flush and brighten with the unmistakable glow of happy love, and she completed Randal's astonishment by running into the arms of the young minister, saying with an irrepressible laugh, "Oh, John, why didn't you come before?"

The court gentleman was all right in a moment, and the coolest of the three as he offered his congratulations and gracefully retired, leaving the lovers to enjoy the tryst he had delayed. But as he went down stairs his brows were knit, and he slapped the broad railing smartly with his cocked hat as if some irritation must find vent in a more energetic way than merely saying, "Confound the little baggage!" under his breath.

Such an amazing supper came from Aunt Plumy's big pantry that the city guests could not eat for laughing at the queer dishes circulating through the rooms, and copiously partaken of by the hearty young folks.

Doughnuts and cheese, pie and pickles, cider and tea, baked beans and custards, cake and cold turkey, bread and butter, plum pudding and French bonbons, Sophie's contribution.

"May I offer you the native delicacies, and share your plate? Both are very good, but the china has run short, and after such vigorous exercise as you have had you must need refreshment. I'm sure I do!" said Randal, bowing before Emily with a great blue platter laden with two doughnuts, two wedges of pumpkin pie and two spoons.

The smile with which she welcomed him, the alacrity with which she made room beside her and seemed to enjoy the supper he brought, was so soothing to his ruffled spirit that he soon began to feel that there is no friend like an old friend, that it would not be difficult to name a sweet woman who would take him in hand and would make him happy if he cared to ask her, and he began to think he would by and by, it was so pleasant to sit in that green corner with waves of crimson brocade flowing over his feet, and a fine face softening beautifully under his eyes.

The supper was not romantic, but the situation was, and Emily found that pie ambrosial food eaten with the man she loved, whose eyes talked more eloquently than the tongue just then busy with a doughnut. Ruth kept away, but glanced at them as she served her company, and her own happy experience helped her to see that all was going well in that quarter. Saul and Sophie emerged from the back entry with shining countenances, but carefully avoided each other for the rest of the evening. No one observed this but Aunt Plumy from the recesses of her pantry, and she folded her hands as if well content, as she murmured fervently over a pan full of crullers, "Bless the dears! Now I can die happy."

Every one thought Sophie's old-fashioned dress immensely becoming, and several of his former men said to Saul with blunt admiration, "Major, you look to-night as you used to after we'd gained a big battle."

"I feel as if I had," answered the splendid Major, with eyes much brighter than his buttons, and a heart under them infinitely prouder than when he was promoted on the field of honor, for his Waterloo was won.

There was more dancing, followed by games, in which Aunt Plumy shone pre-eminent, for the supper was off her mind and she could enjoy herself. There were shouts of merriment as the blithe old lady twirled the platter, hunted the squirrel, and went to Jerusalem like a girl of sixteen; her cap in a ruinous condition, and every seam of the purple dress straining like sails in a gale. It was great fun, but at midnight it came to an end, and the young folks, still bubbling over with innocent jollity, went jingling away along the snowy hills, unanimously pronouncing Mrs. Basset's party the best of the season.

"Never had such a good time in my life!" exclaimed Sophie, as the family stood together in the kitchen where the candles among the wreaths were going out, and the floor was strewn with wrecks of past joy.

"I'm proper glad, dear. Now you all go to bed and lay as late as you like to-morrow. I'm so kinder worked up I couldn't sleep, so Saul and me will put things to rights without a mite of noise to disturb you"; and Aunt Plumy sent them off with a smile that was a benediction, Sophie thought.

"The dear old soul speaks as if midnight was an un-heard-of hour for Christians to be up. What would she say if she knew how we seldom go to bed till dawn in the ball season? I'm so wide awake I've half a mind to pack a little. Randal must go at two, he says, and we shall want his escort," said Emily, as the girls laid away their brocades in the press in Sophie's room.

"I'm not going. Aunt can't spare me, and there is nothing to go for yet," answered Sophie, beginning to take the white chrysanthemums out of her pretty hair.

"My dear child, you will die of ennui up here. Very nice for a week or so, but frightful for a winter. We are going to be very gay, and cannot get on without you," cried Emily dismayed at the suggestion.

"You will have to, for I'm not coming. I am very happy here, and so tired of the frivolous life I lead in town, that I have decided to try a better one," and Sophie's mirror reflected a face full of the sweetest content.

"Have you lost your mind? experienced religion? or any other dreadful thing? You always were odd, but this last freak is the strangest of all. What will your guardian say, and the world?" added Emily in the awe-stricken tone of one who stood in fear of the omnipotent Mrs. Grundy.

"Guardy will be glad to be rid of me, and I don't care that for the world," cried Sophie, snapping her fingers with a joyful sort of recklessness which completed Emily's bewilderment.

"But Mr. Hammond? Are you going to throw away millions, lose your chance of making the best match in the city, and driving the girls of our set out of their wits with envy?"

Sophie laughed at her friend's despairing cry, and turning round said quietly,—

"I wrote to Mr. Hammond last night, and this evening received my reward for being an honest girl. Saul and I are to be married in the spring when Ruth is."

Emily fell prone upon the bed as if the announcement was too much for her, but was up again in an instant to declare with prophetic solemnity,—

"I knew something was going on, but hoped to get you away before you were lost. Sophie, you will repent. Be warned, and forget this sad delusion."

"Too late for that. The pang I suffered yesterday when I thought Saul was dead showed me how well I loved him. To-night he asked me to stay, and no power in the world can part us. Oh! Emily, it is all so sweet, so beautiful, that everything is possible, and I know I shall be happy in this dear old home, full of love and peace and honest hearts. I only hope you may find as true and tender a man to live for as my Saul."

Sophie's face was more eloquent than her fervent words, and Emily beautifully illustrated the inconsistency of her sex by suddenly embracing her friend, with the incoherent exclamation, "I think I have, dear! Your brave Saul is worth a dozen old Hammonds, and I do believe you are right."

It is unnecessary to tell how, as if drawn by the irresistible magic of sympathy, Ruth and her mother crept in one by one to join the midnight conference and add their smiles and tears, tender hopes and proud delight to the joys of that memorable hour. Nor how Saul, unable to sleep, mounted guard below, and meeting Randal prowling down to soothe his nerves with a surreptitious cigar found it impossible to help confiding to his attentive ear the happiness that would break bounds and overflow in unusual eloquence.

Peace fell upon the old house at last, and all slept as if some magic herb had touched their eyelids, bringing blissful dreams and a glad awakening.

"Can't we persuade you to come with us, Miss Sophie?" asked Randal next day, as they made their adieux.

"I'm under orders now, and dare not disobey my superior officer," answered Sophie, handing her Major his driving gloves, with a look which plainly showed that she had joined the great army of devoted women who enlist for life and ask no pay but love.

"I shall depend on being invited to your wedding, then, and yours, too, Miss Ruth," added Randal, shaking hands with "the little baggage," as if he had quite forgiven her mockery and forgotten his own brief lapse into sentiment.

Before she could reply Aunt Plumy said, in a tone of

calm conviction, that made them all laugh, and some of them look conscious,—

"Spring is a good time for weddin's, and I shouldn't wonder ef there was quite a number."

"Nor I"; and Saul and Sophie smiled at one another as they saw how carefully Randal arranged Emily's wraps.

Then with kisses, thanks and all the good wishes that happy hearts could imagine, the guests drove away, to remember long and gratefully that pleasant country Christmas.

WHEN CHRISTMAS COMES

Libbie C. Baer

(HARRY.)

When Christmas comes my brother Fred
And I are each to have a sled,
So papa says. To all *good* boys
Old Santa brings both books and toys,
    When Christmas comes.

(PAUL.)

I know my mother is too poor,
To buy us toys, but I am sure

She'll have for us some nice warm caps,
Some mittens, and some shoes, perhaps,
    When Christmas comes.

(JAMES.)

I wrote old Santa Claus to bring
To me a drum, and everything;
A train of cars to run by steam,
And all of which I think, and dream,
    When Christmas comes.

(WILLIE.)

You greedy boy! You want it all;
I only want a top and ball;
I want what Santa Claus can spare
When *other* boys have had their share,
    When Christmas comes.

(JAMES.)

I only wrote old Santa Claus
To bring me all those things, because

I want to *give away* some toys,
To *Paul*, and other widows' boys,
    When Christmas comes.

(JOHN.)

That's right, my chum,
With fife and drum,
And singing tops we'll make things hum;
Divide our toys with other boys,
And won't we make a sight of noise,
    When Christmas comes.

(ALL.)

When Christmas comes to you and me,
Bid every selfish thought to flee;
Unselfish hearts and deeds, and then,
"Peace on earth, good will to men,"
    When Christmas comes.